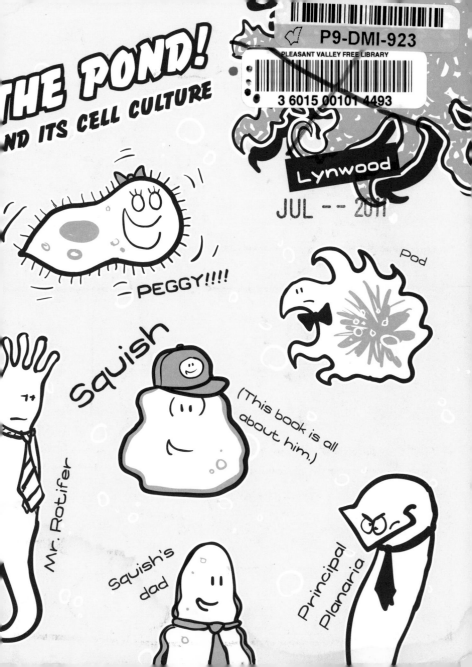

THE POND!
AND ITS CELL CULTURE

PEGGY!!!!

Pod

Squish

(This book is all about him.)

Mr. Rotifer

Squish's dad

Principal Planaria

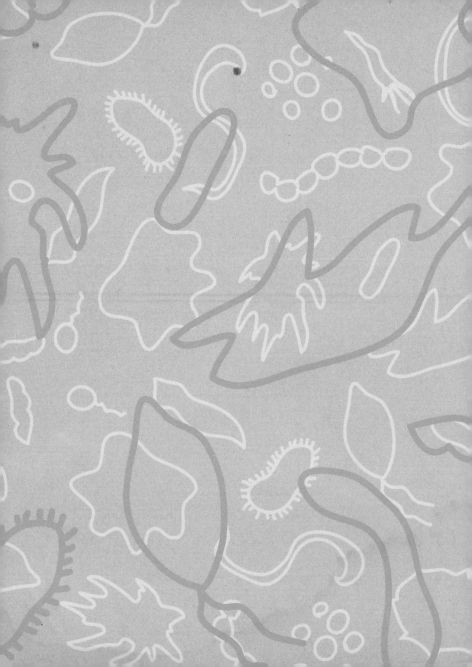

squish

SUPER AMOEBA

BY JENNIFER L. HOLM & MATTHEW HOLM

RANDOM HOUSE NEW YORK

Published in the United States by
Random House Children's Books,
a division of Random House, Inc., New York.
Random House and the colophon are
registered trademarks of Random House, Inc.

Visit us on the Web! www.randomhouse.com/kids
Educators and librarians, for a variety of teaching tools,
visit us at www.randomhouse.com/teachers

Library of Congress Cataloging-in-Publication Data
Holm, Jennifer L.
Squish, Super Amoeba / by Jennifer L. Holm and
Matthew Holm. – 1st ed. p. cm.
Summary: Squish, a meek amoeba who loves the comic book exploits of his favorite hero, "Super Amoeba," tries to emulate him when his best friend is threatened by a bully.
ISBN 978-0-375-84389-1 (trade) –
ISBN 978-0-375-93783-5 (lib. bdg.)
1. Graphic novels. [1. Graphic novels. 2. Amoeba–Fiction.
3. Schools–Fiction. 4. Bullies–Fiction. 5. Courage–Fiction.
6. Superheroes–Fiction.] I. Holm, Matthew. II. Title.
III. Title: Super Amoeba.
PZ7.7.H65Sq 2011 741.5'973–dc22 2010008004

MANUFACTURED IN MALAYSIA 10 9 8 7 6 5 4 3 2 1
First Edition

Random House Children's Books supports the First Amendment and celebrates the right to read.

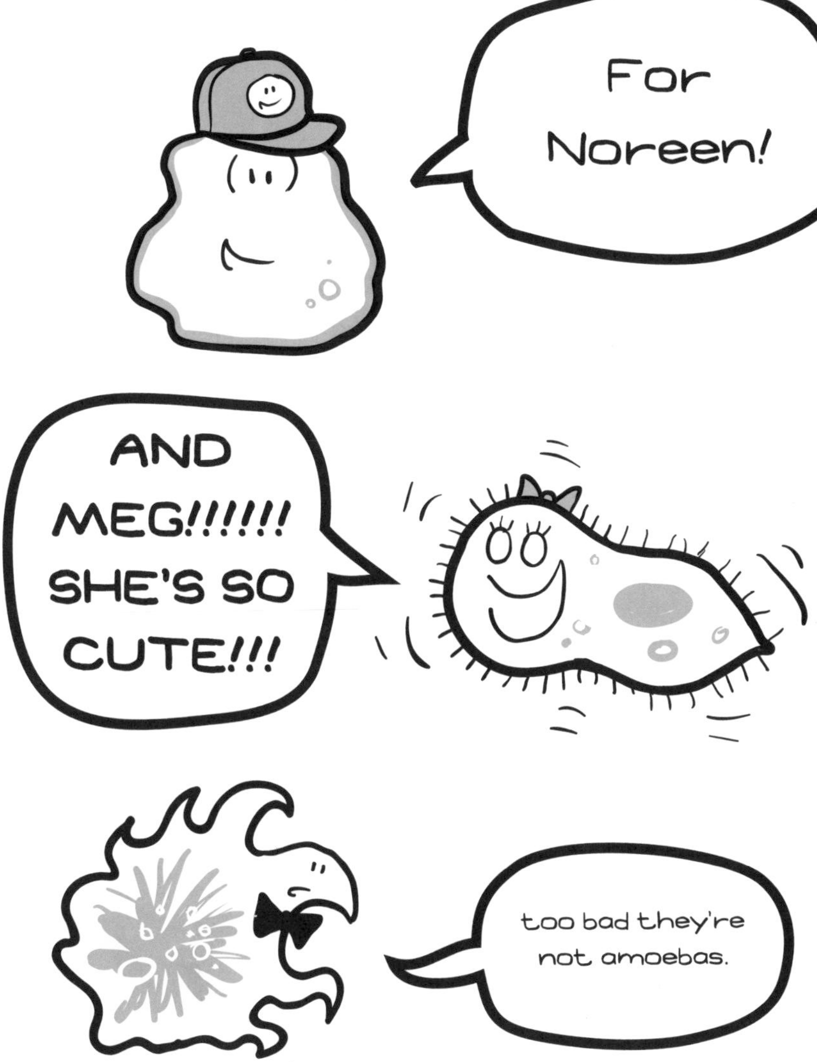
For Noreen!
AND MEG!!!!!!! SHE'S SO CUTE!!!
too bad they're not amoebas.

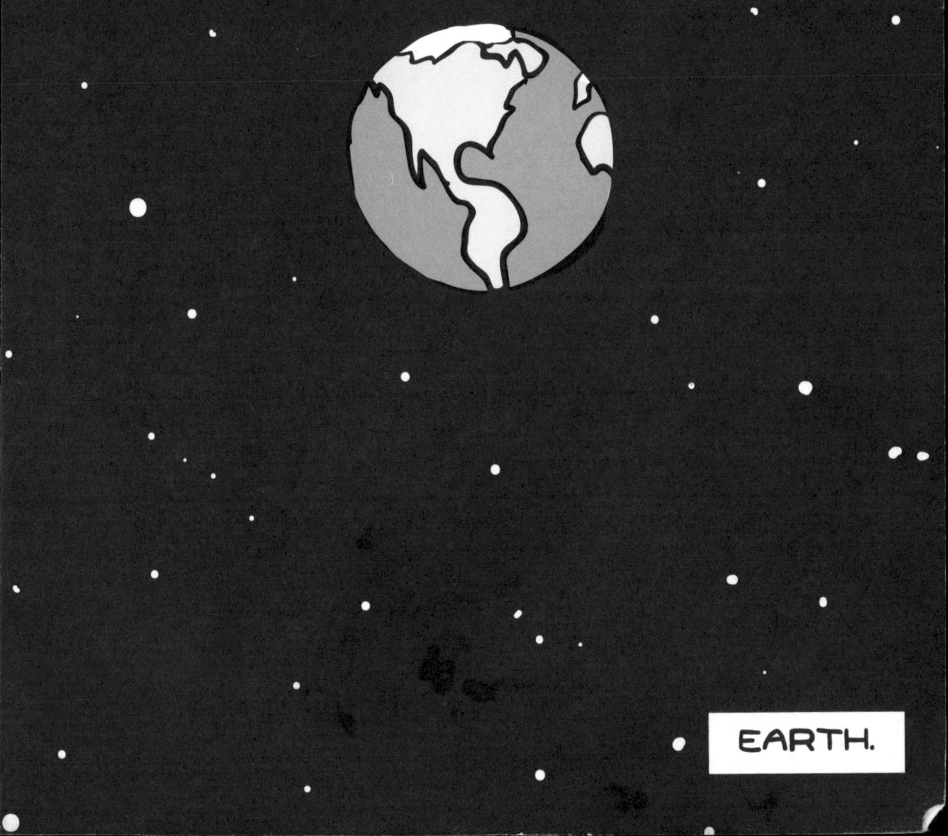
EARTH.

OUR PLANET HOSTS A RICH DIVERSITY OF LIFE . . .

FROM LUSH RAIN FORESTS TO DRY DESERTS.

BUT BENEATH THIS WORLD LIES ANOTHER ONE.

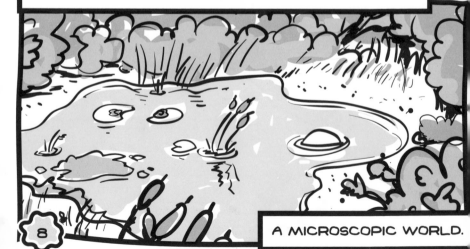

A MICROSCOPIC WORLD.

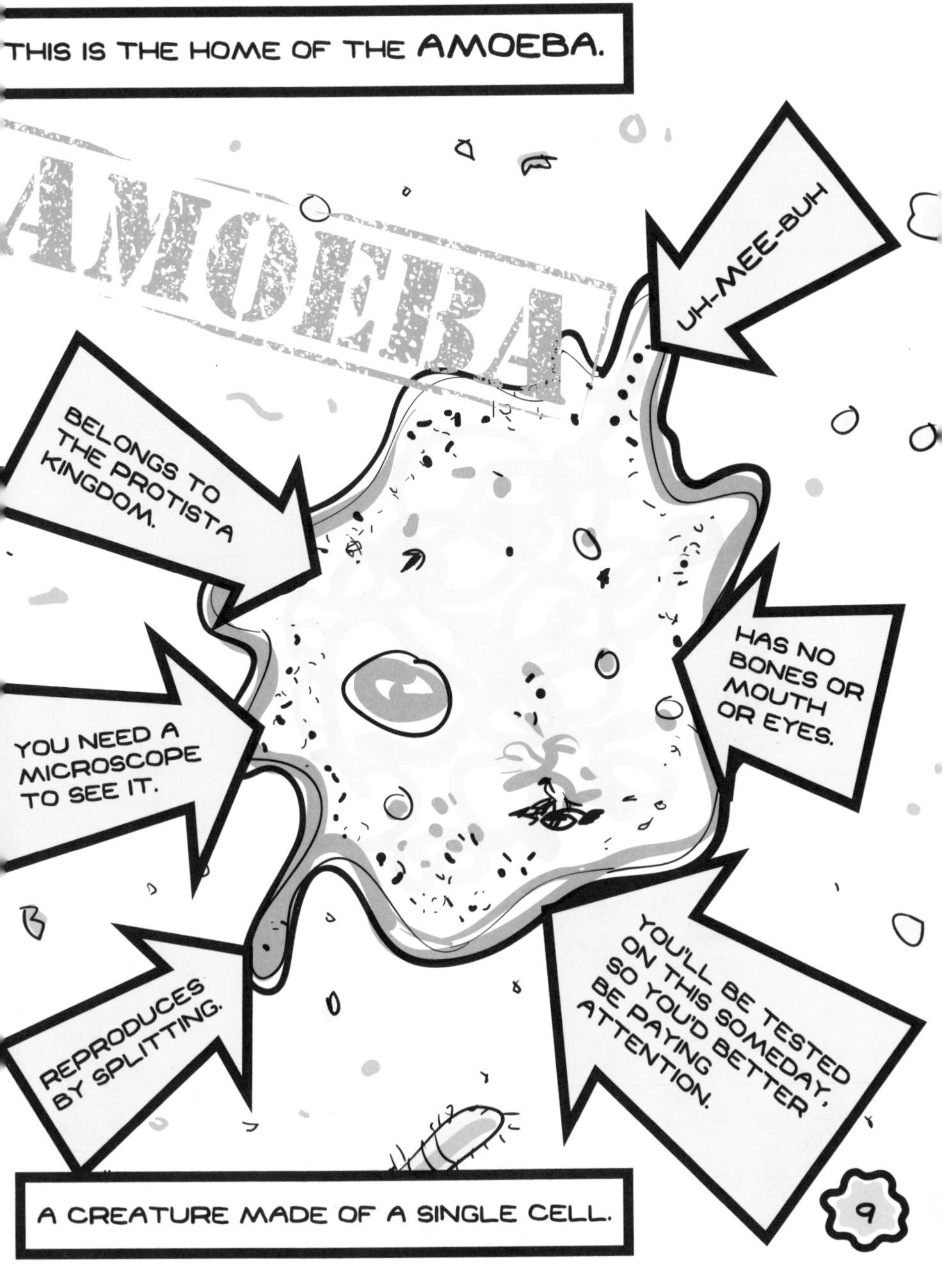
THIS IS THE HOME OF THE AMOEBA.
AMOEBA
UH-MEE-BUH
BELONGS TO THE PROTISTA KINGDOM.
HAS NO BONES OR MOUTH OR EYES.
YOU NEED A MICROSCOPE TO SEE IT.
REPRODUCES BY SPLITTING.
YOU'LL BE TESTED ON THIS SOMEDAY, SO YOU'D BETTER BE PAYING ATTENTION.
A CREATURE MADE OF A SINGLE CELL.

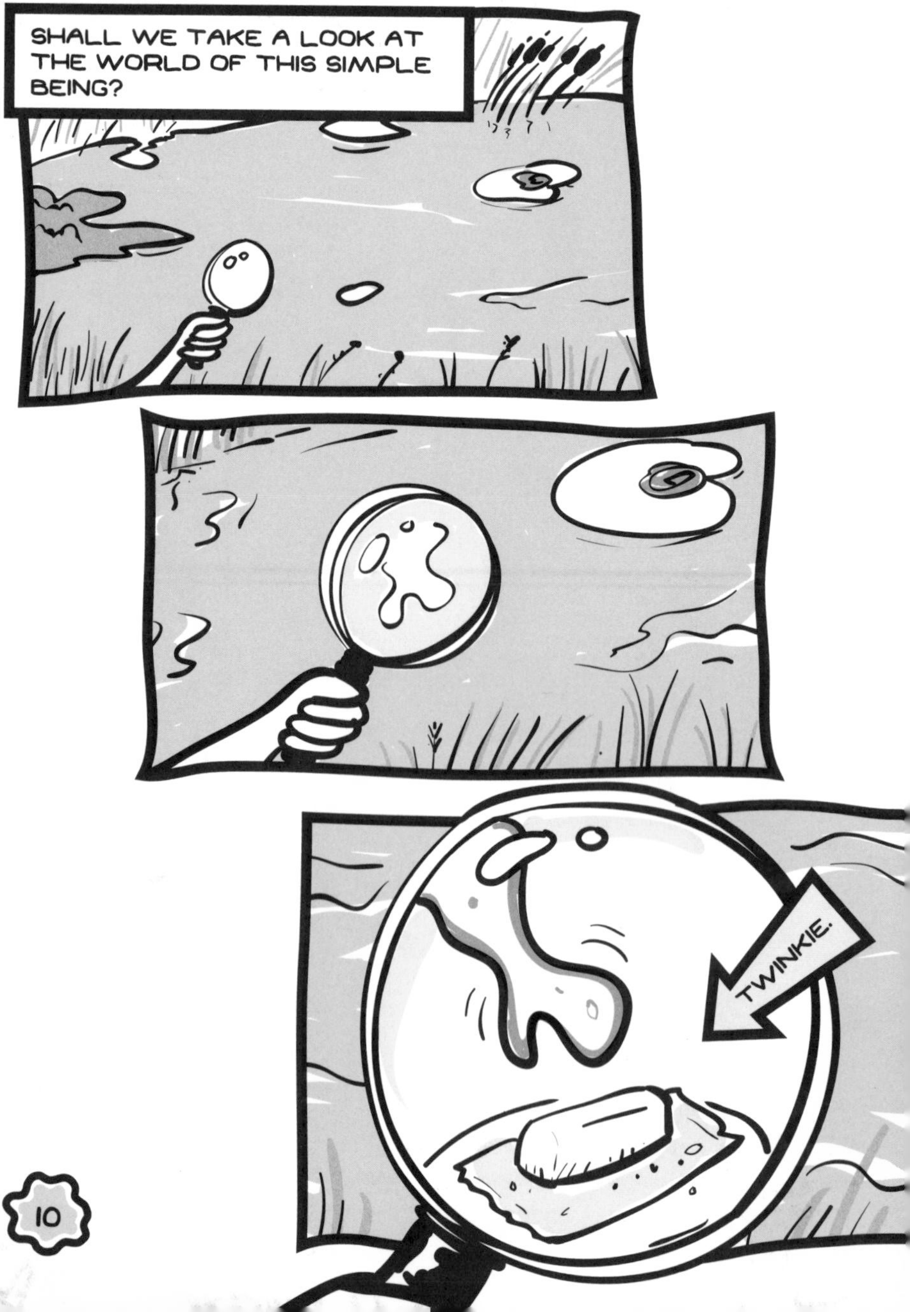
SHALL WE TAKE A LOOK AT THE WORLD OF THIS SIMPLE BEING?
TWINKIE.

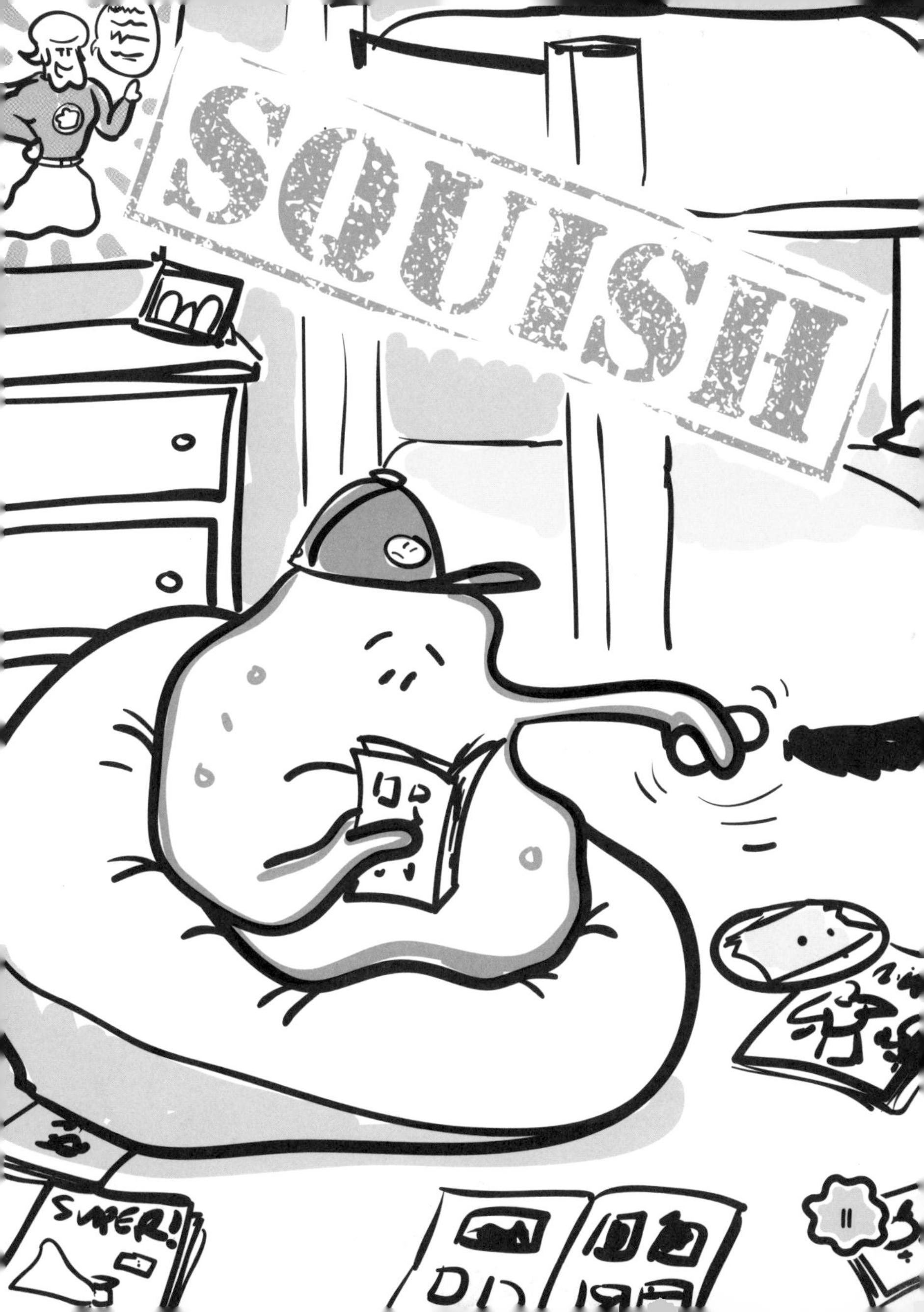
SQUISH
SUPER!

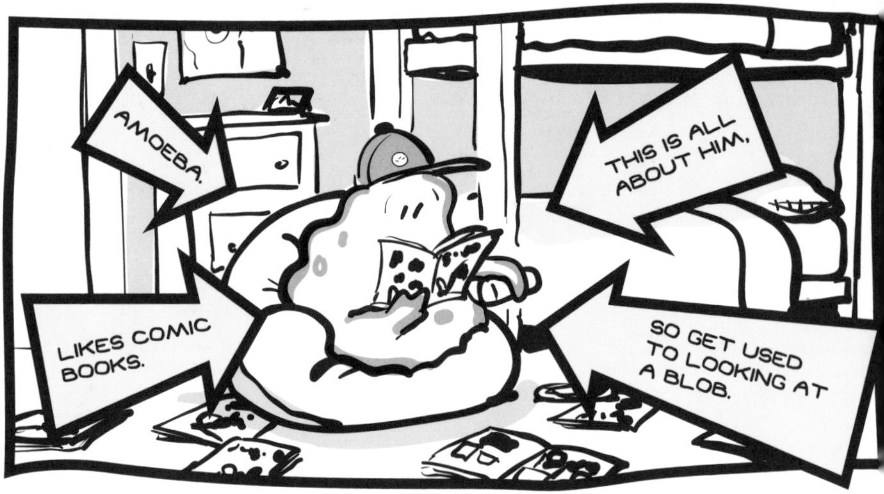
AMOEBA.
THIS IS ALL ABOUT HIM.
LIKES COMIC BOOKS.
SO GET USED TO LOOKING AT A BLOB.

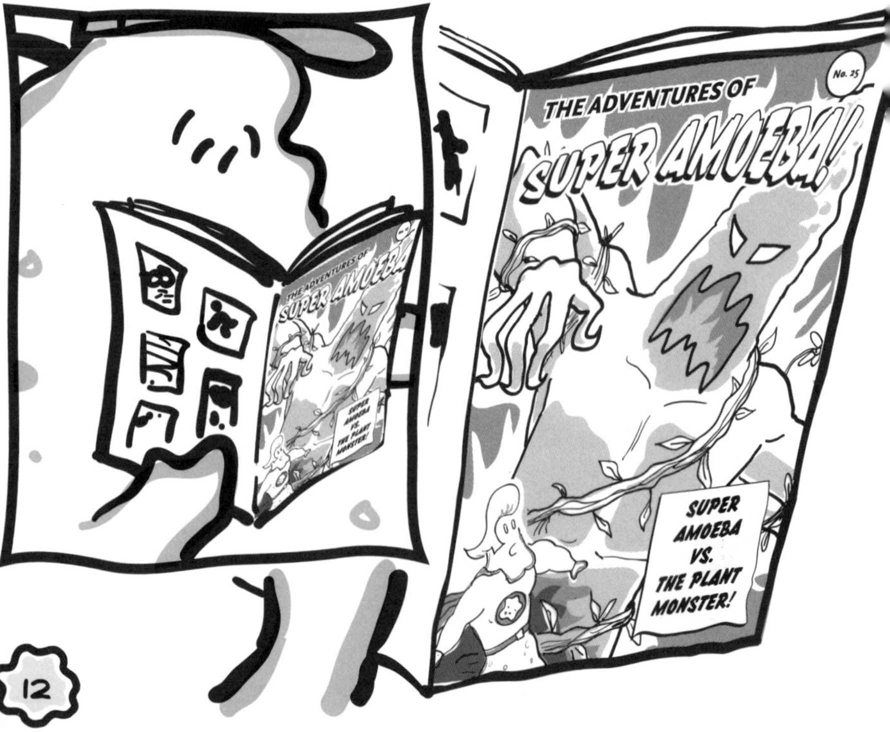
No. 25
THE ADVENTURES OF
SUPER AMOEBA!
SUPER AMOEBA VS. THE PLANT MONSTER!

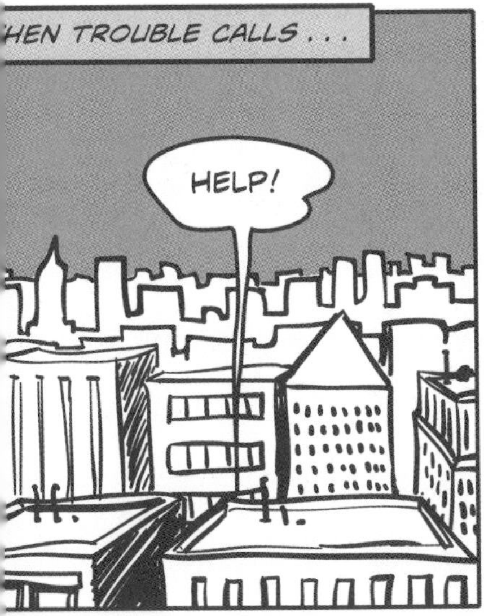
HEN TROUBLE CALLS . . .
HELP!

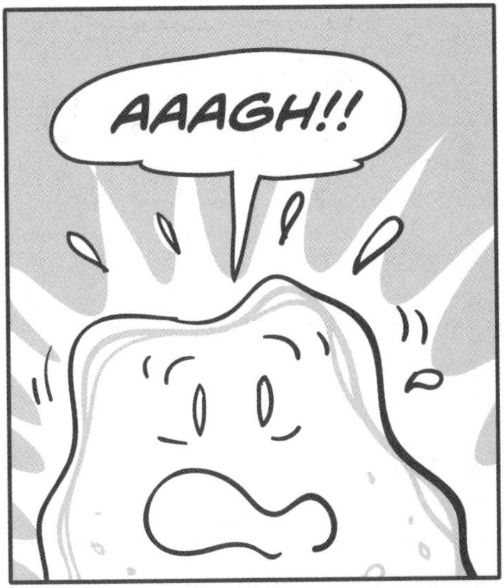
AAAGH!!

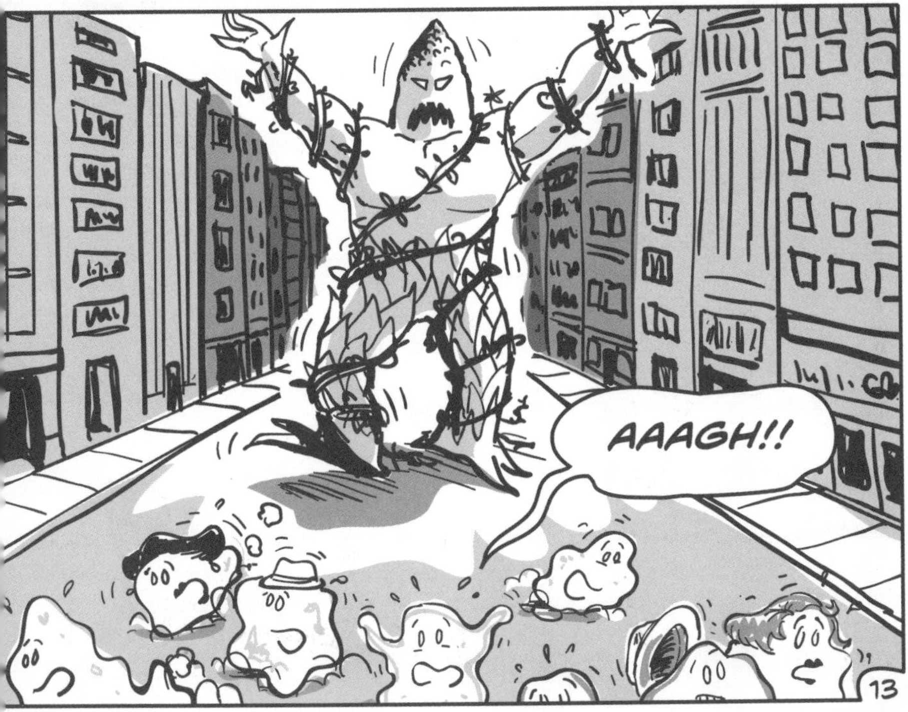
AAAGH!!

THERE IS A SINGLE CELL . . .

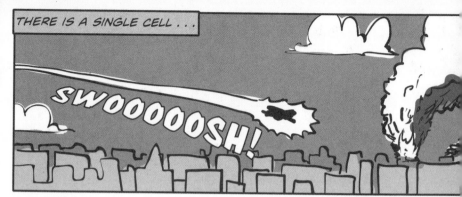

SWOOOOOSH!

PLUCK

WALIGH!

SLURP!

14

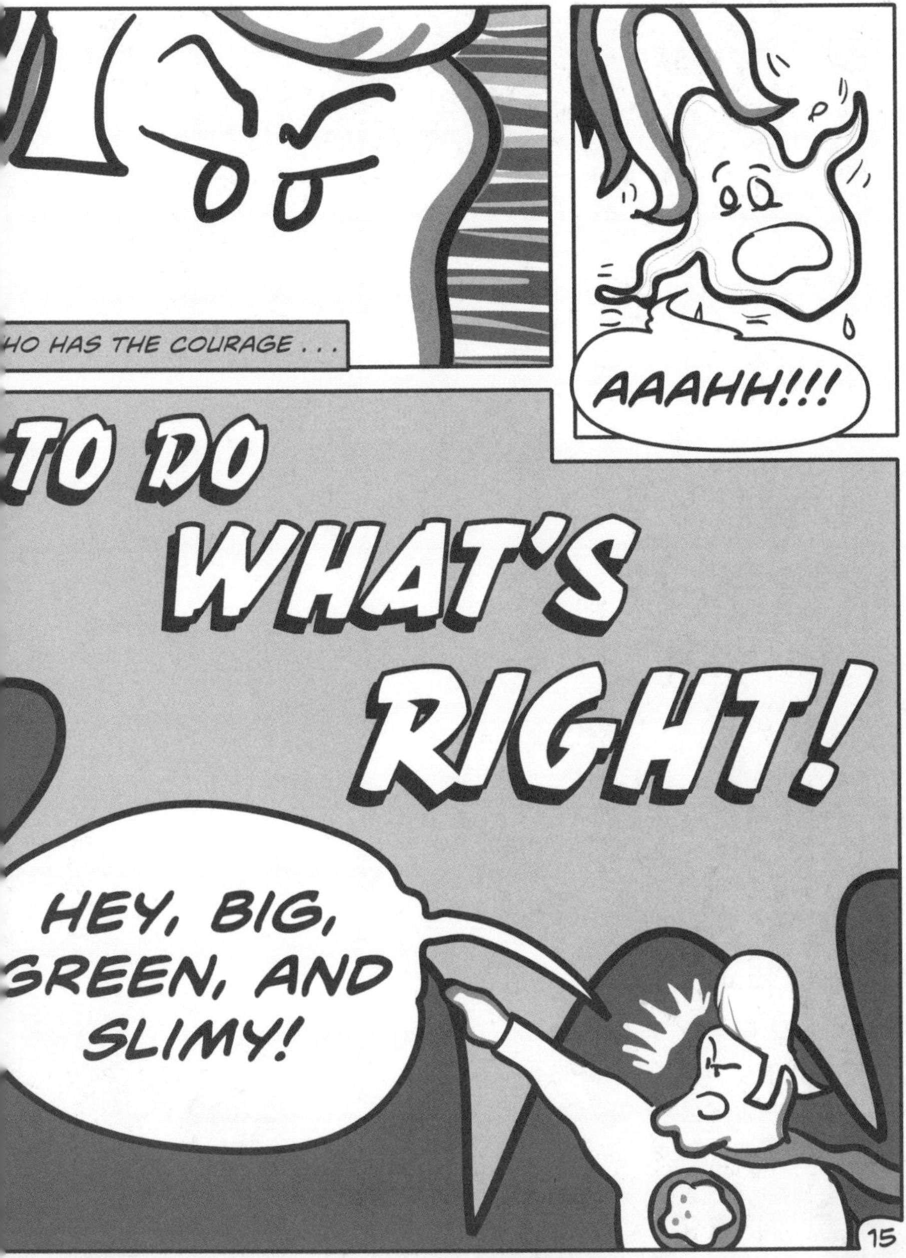

HO HAS THE COURAGE . . .
AAAHH!!!
TO DO WHAT'S RIGHT!
HEY, BIG, GREEN, AND SLIMY!

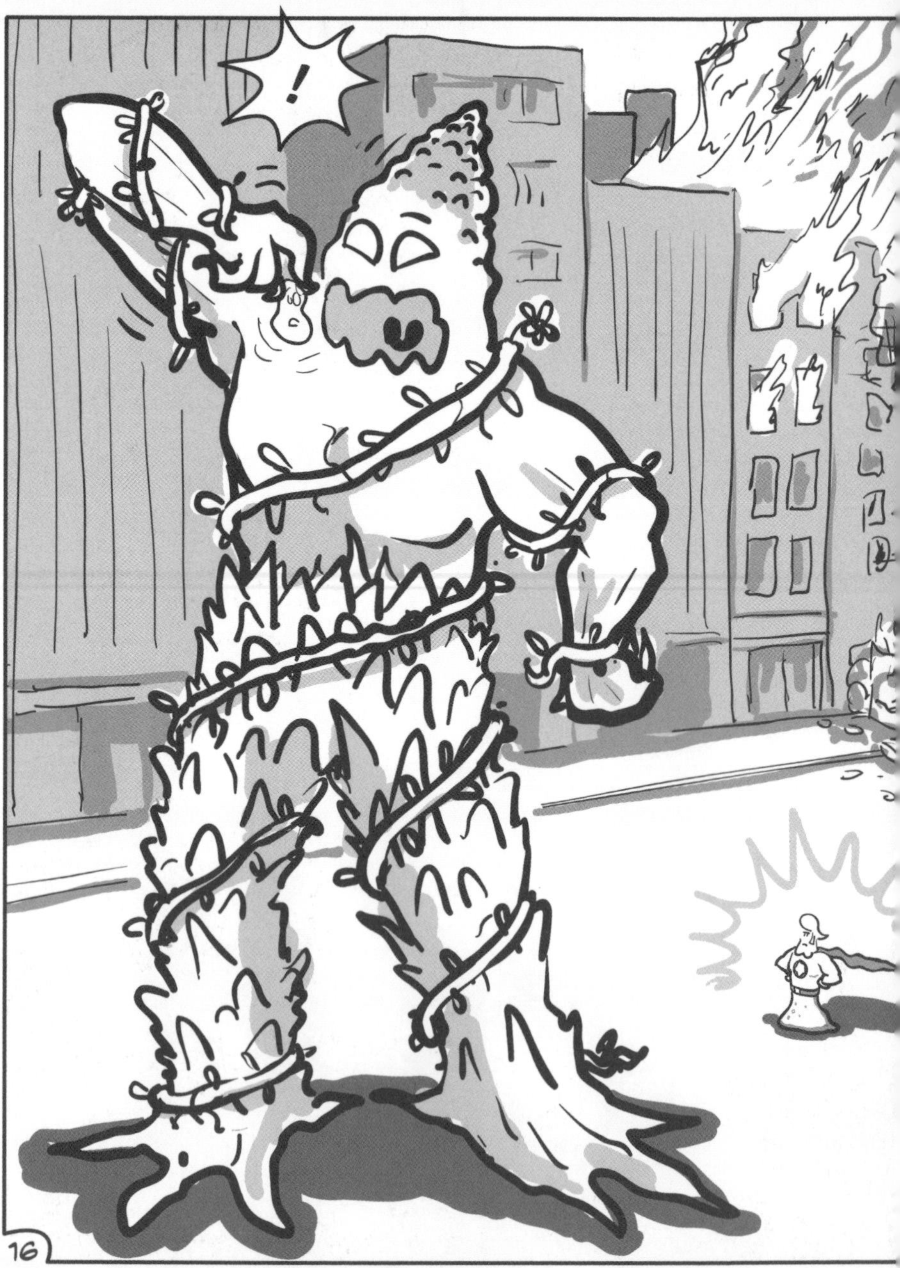
!

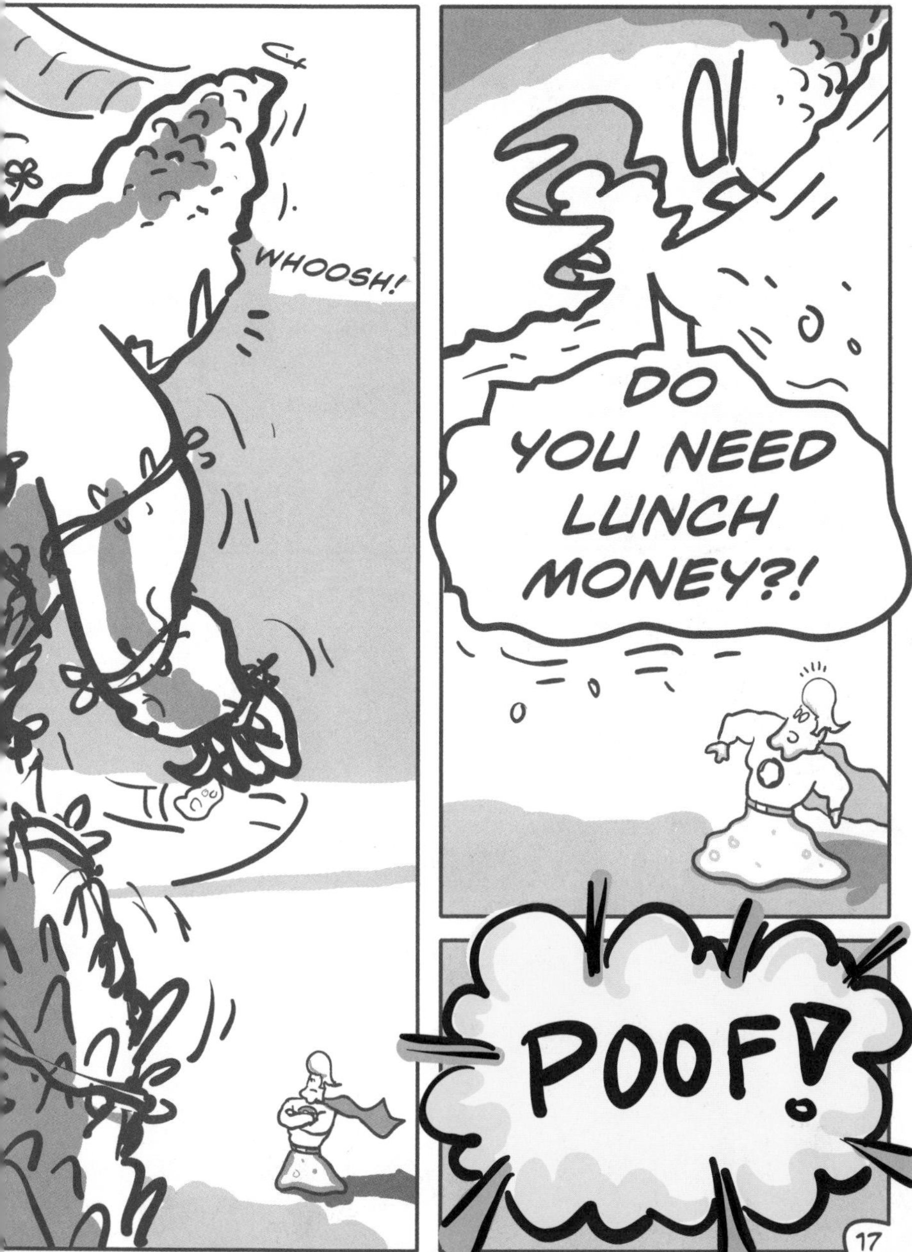
WHOOSH!
DO YOU NEED LUNCH MONEY?!
POOF!

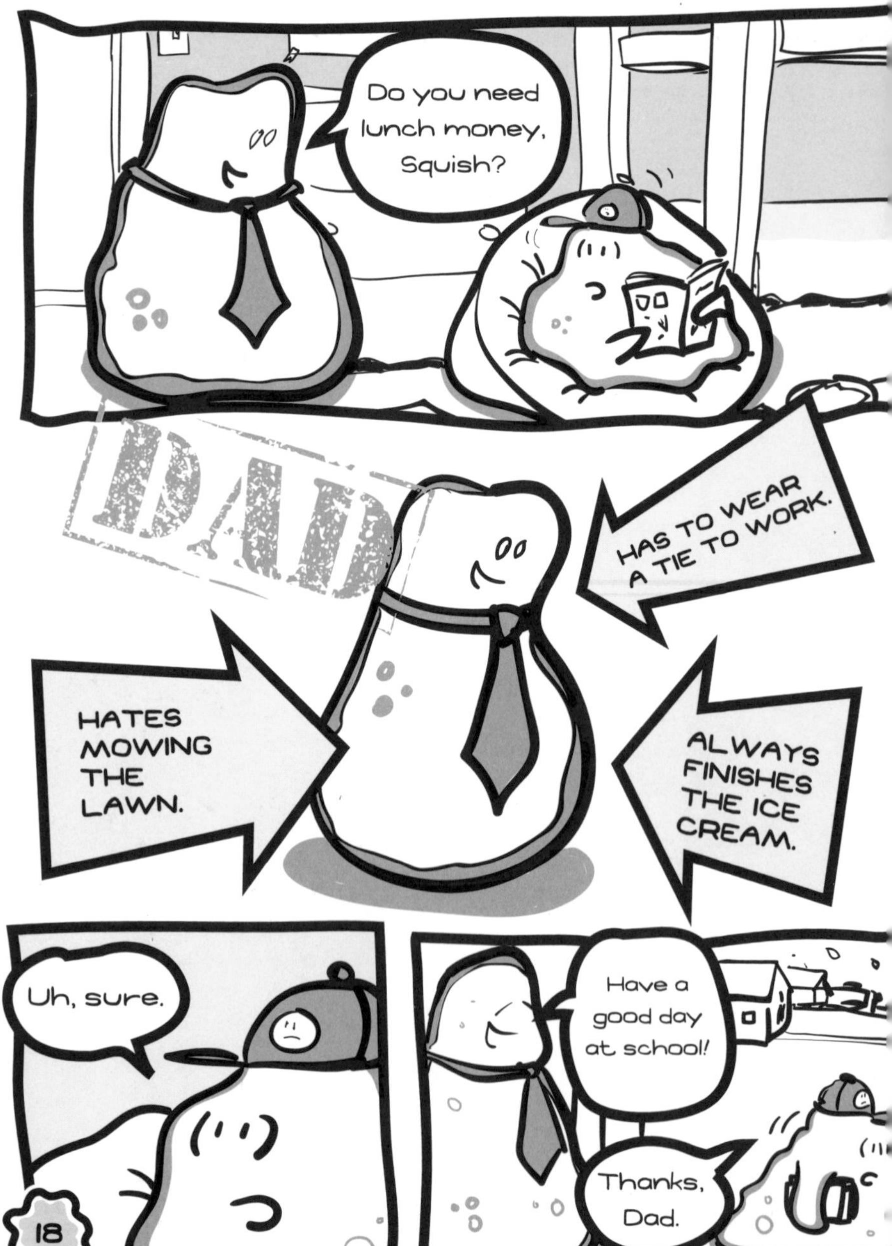
Do you need lunch money, Squish?
DAD
HAS TO WEAR A TIE TO WORK.
HATES MOWING THE LAWN.
ALWAYS FINISHES THE ICE CREAM.
Uh, sure.
Have a good day at school!
Thanks, Dad.

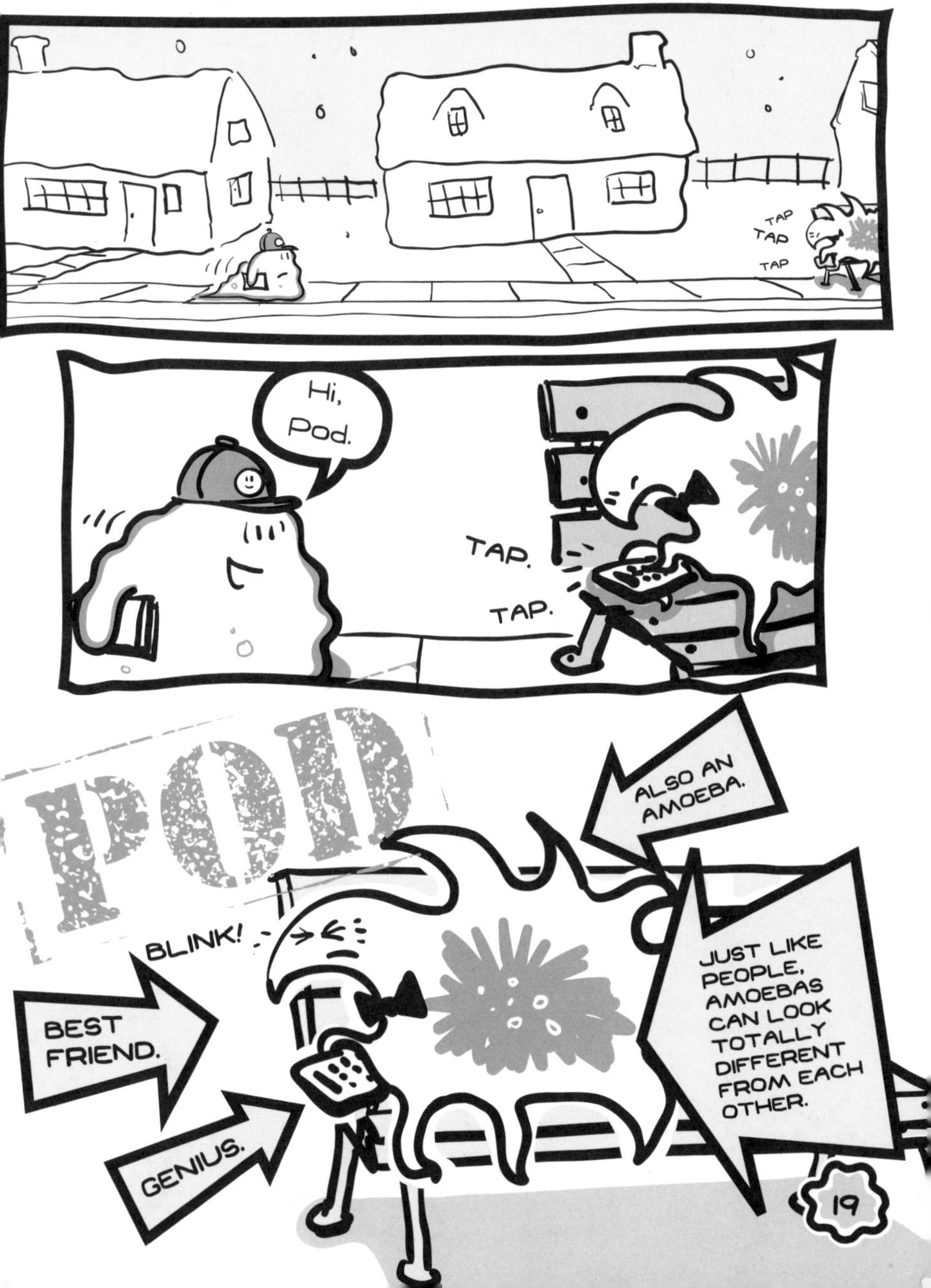
TAP
TAP
TAP
Hi, Pod.
TAP.
TAP.
POD
ALSO AN AMOEBA.
BLINK!
JUST LIKE PEOPLE, AMOEBAS CAN LOOK TOTALLY DIFFERENT FROM EACH OTHER.
BEST FRIEND.
GENIUS.

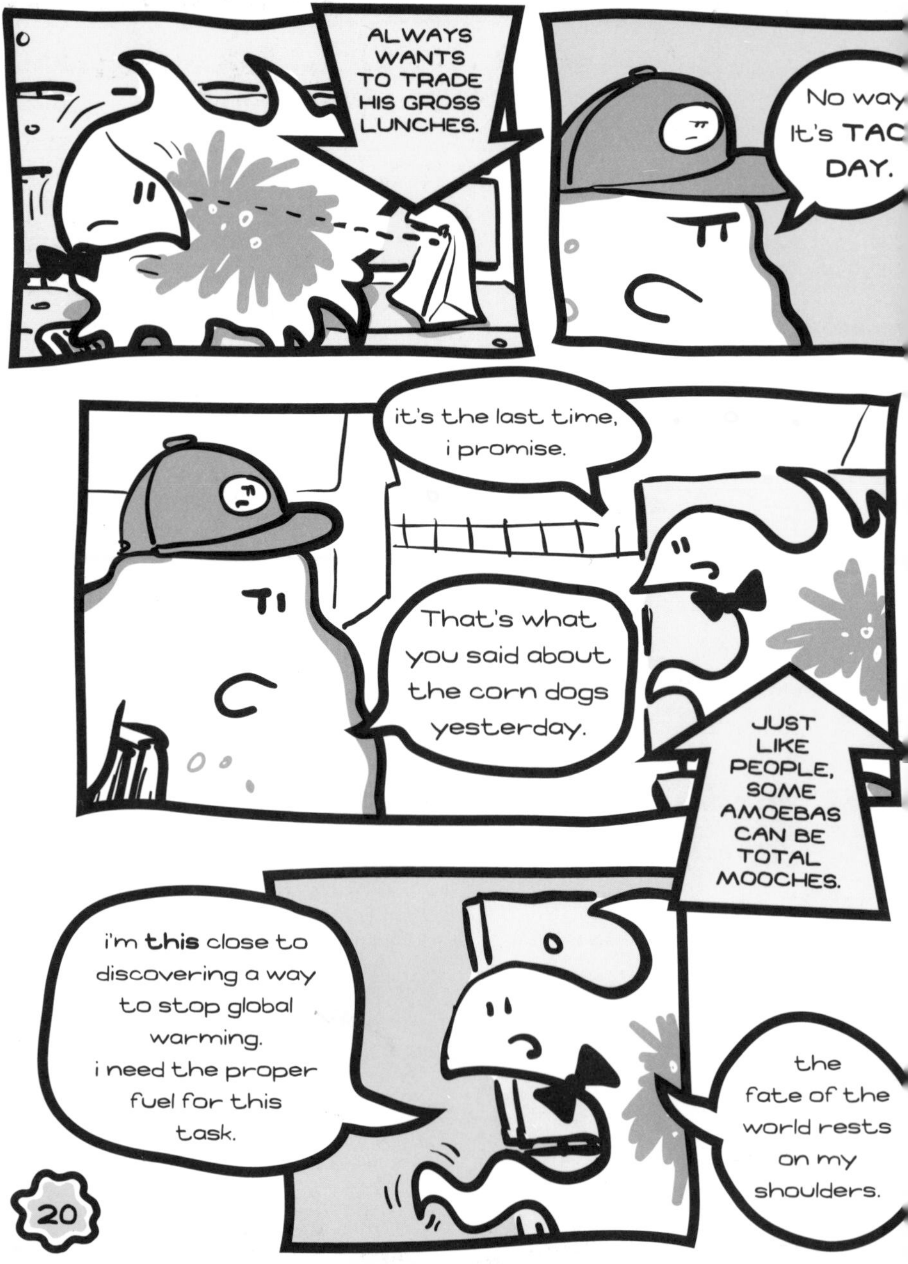
ALWAYS WANTS TO TRADE HIS GROSS LUNCHES.
No way. It's TACO DAY.
it's the last time, i promise.
That's what you said about the corn dogs yesterday.
JUST LIKE PEOPLE, SOME AMOEBAS CAN BE TOTAL MOOCHES.
i'm **this** close to discovering a way to stop global warming. i need the proper fuel for this task.
the fate of the world rests on my shoulders.

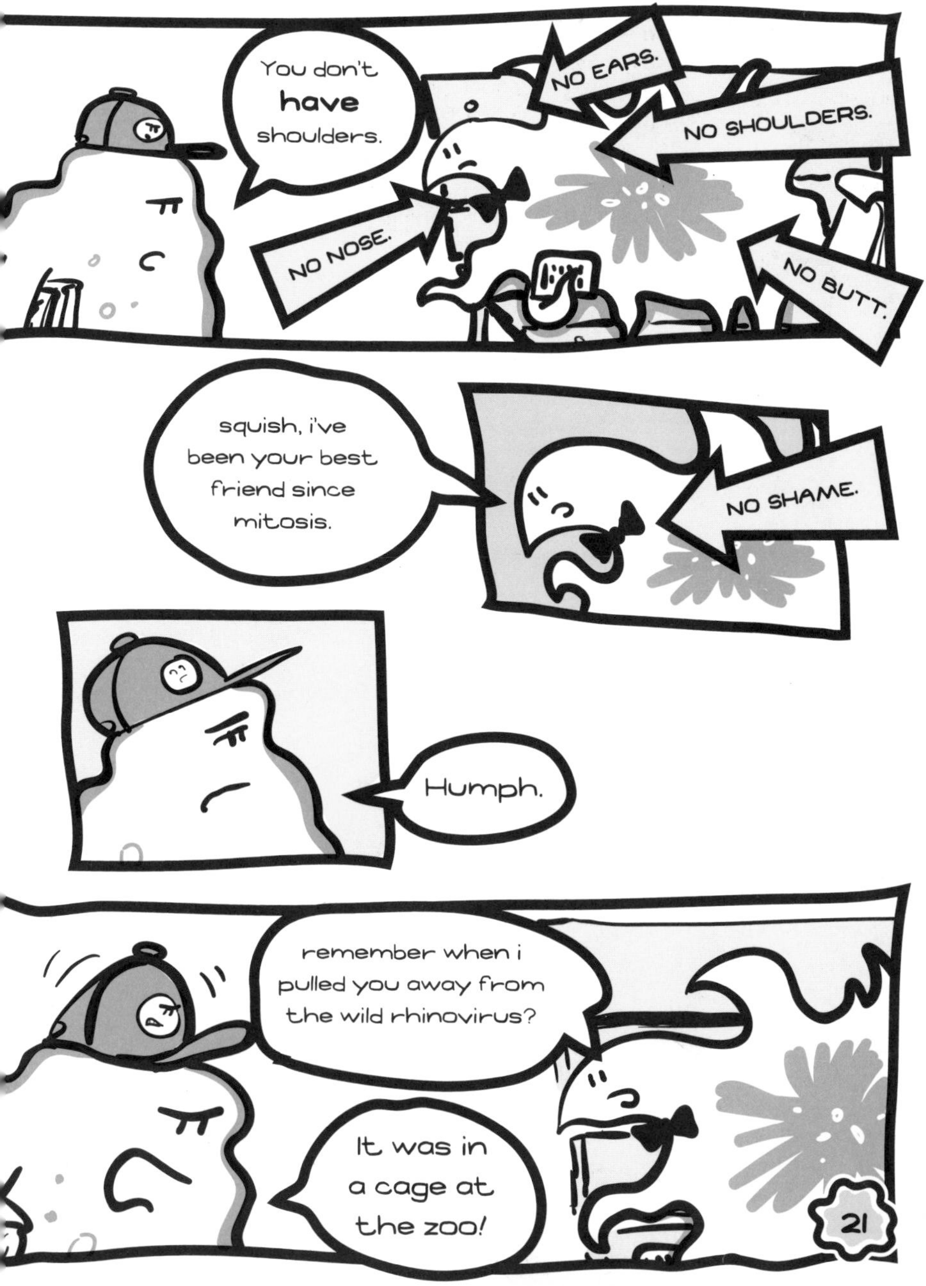
You don't **have** shoulders.
NO EARS.
NO SHOULDERS.
NO NOSE.
NO BUTT.
squish, i've been your best friend since mitosis.
NO SHAME.
Humph.
remember when i pulled you away from the wild rhinovirus?
It was in a cage at the zoo!
21

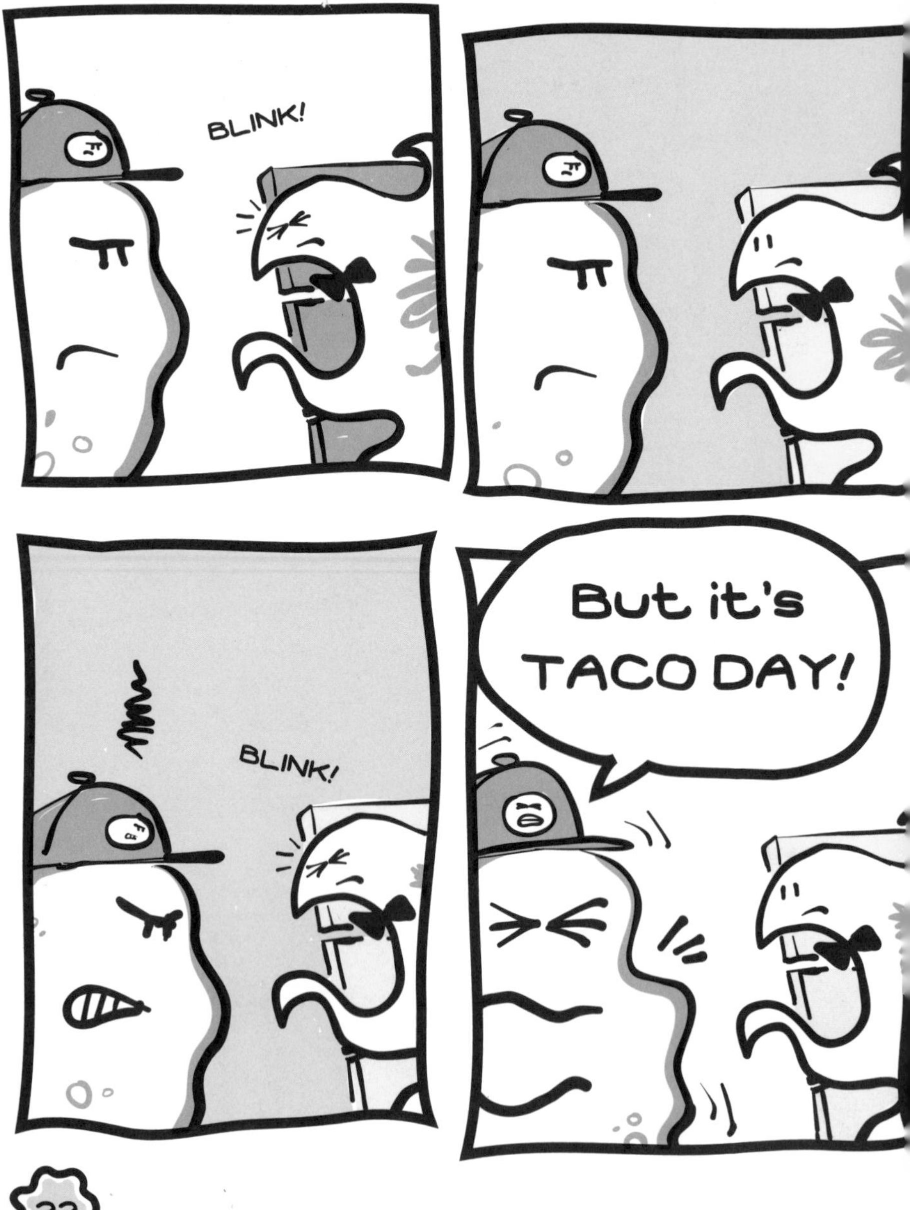
BLINK!
BLINK!
But it's TACO DAY!

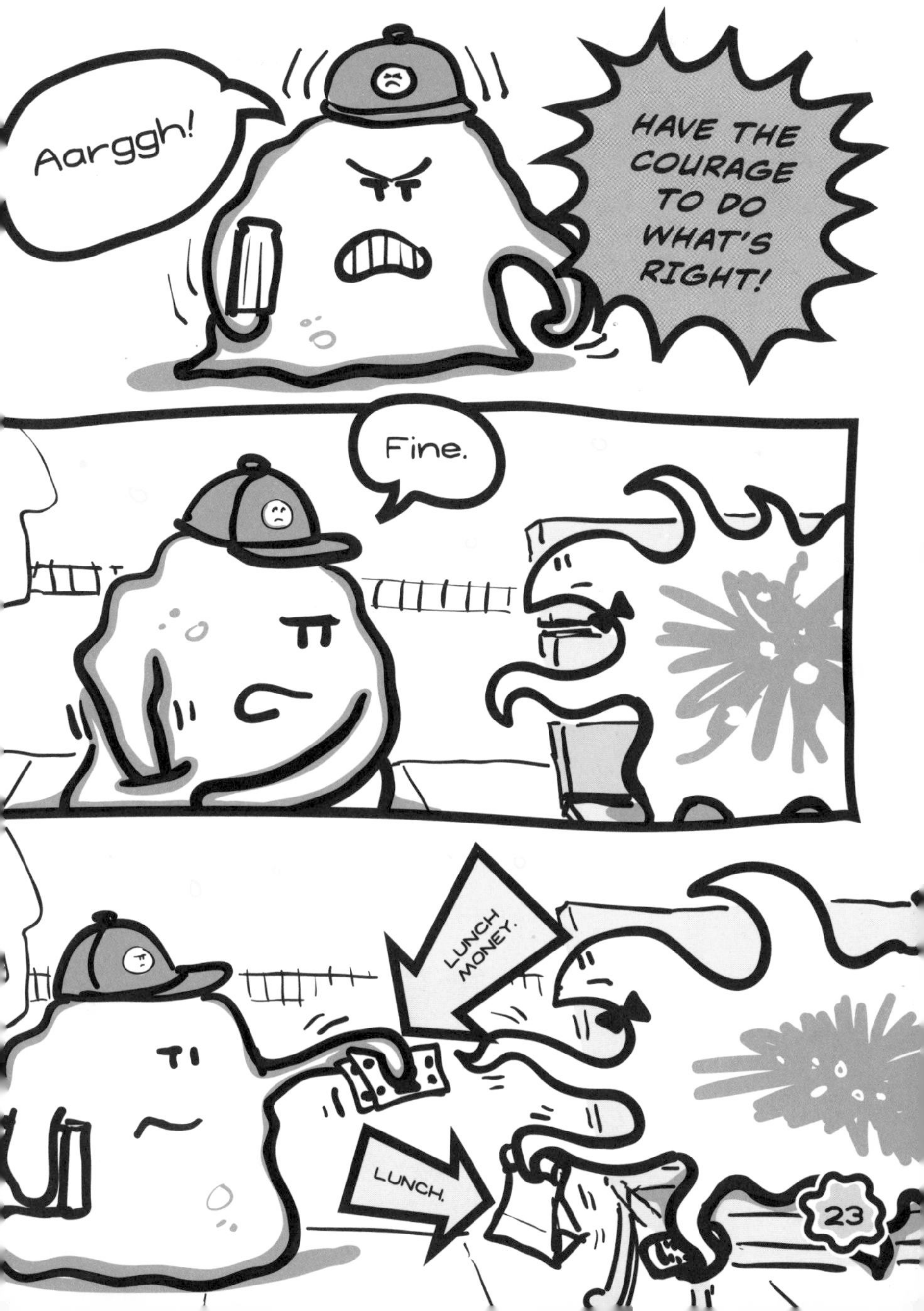
Aarggh!
HAVE THE COURAGE TO DO WHAT'S RIGHT!
Fine.
LUNCH MONEY.
LUNCH.
23

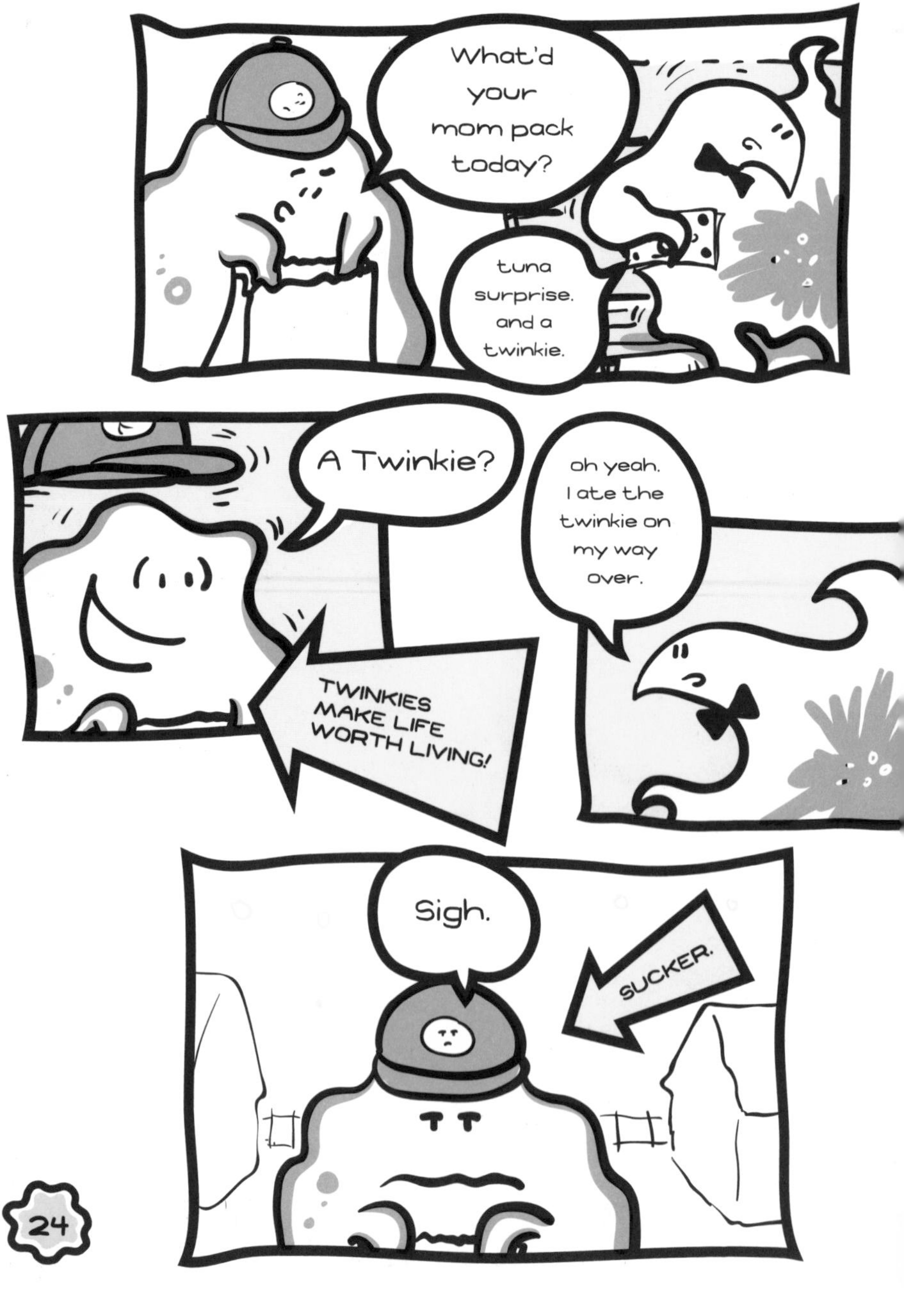
What'd your mom pack today?
tuna surprise. and a twinkie.
A Twinkie?
TWINKIES MAKE LIFE WORTH LIVING!
oh yeah. I ate the twinkie on my way over.
Sigh.
SUCKER.

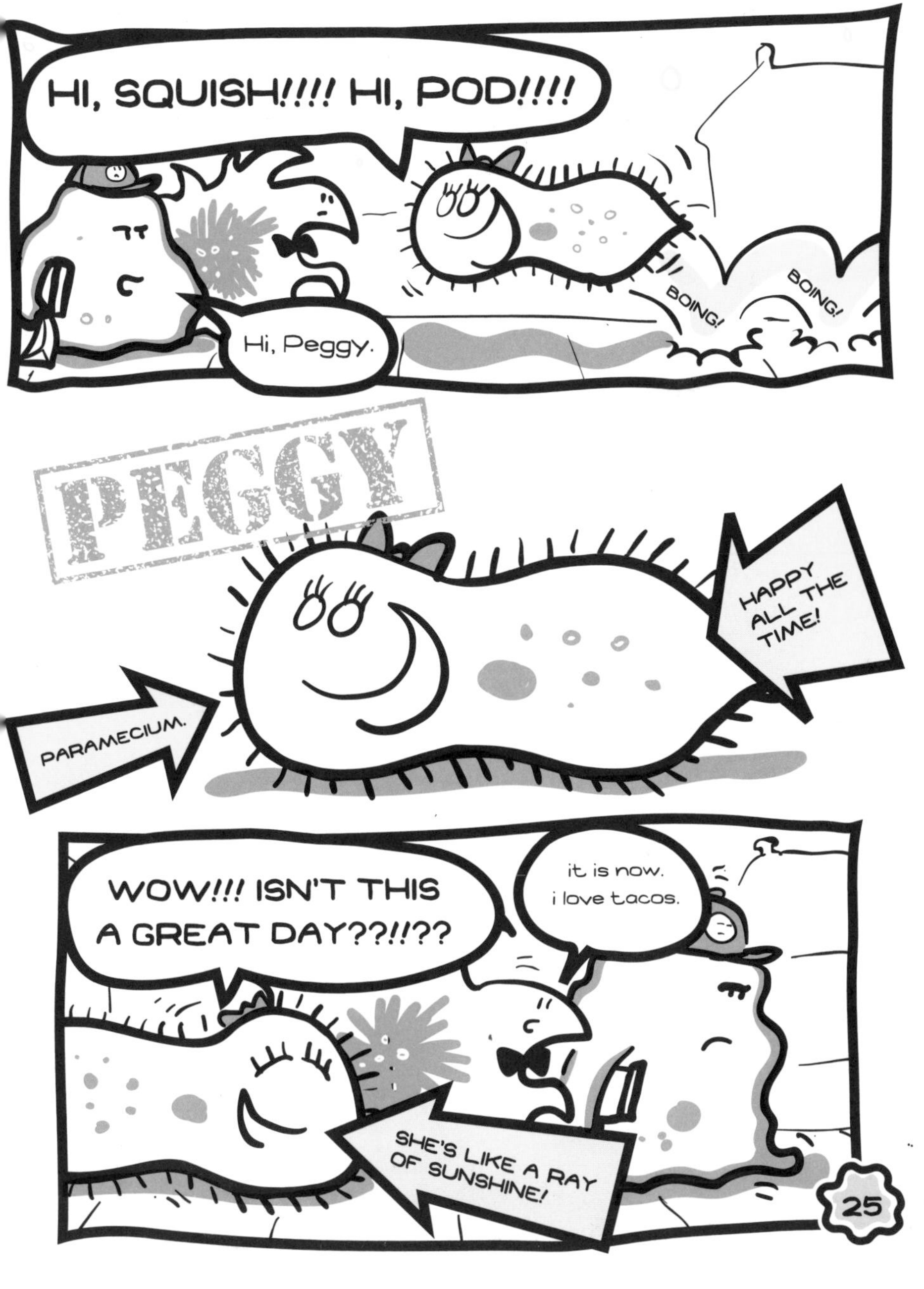
HI, SQUISH!!!! HI, POD!!!!
Hi, Peggy.
BOING!
BOING!
PEGGY
PARAMECIUM.
HAPPY ALL THE TIME!
WOW!!! ISN'T THIS A GREAT DAY??!!??
it is now. i love tacos.
SHE'S LIKE A RAY OF SUNSHINE!

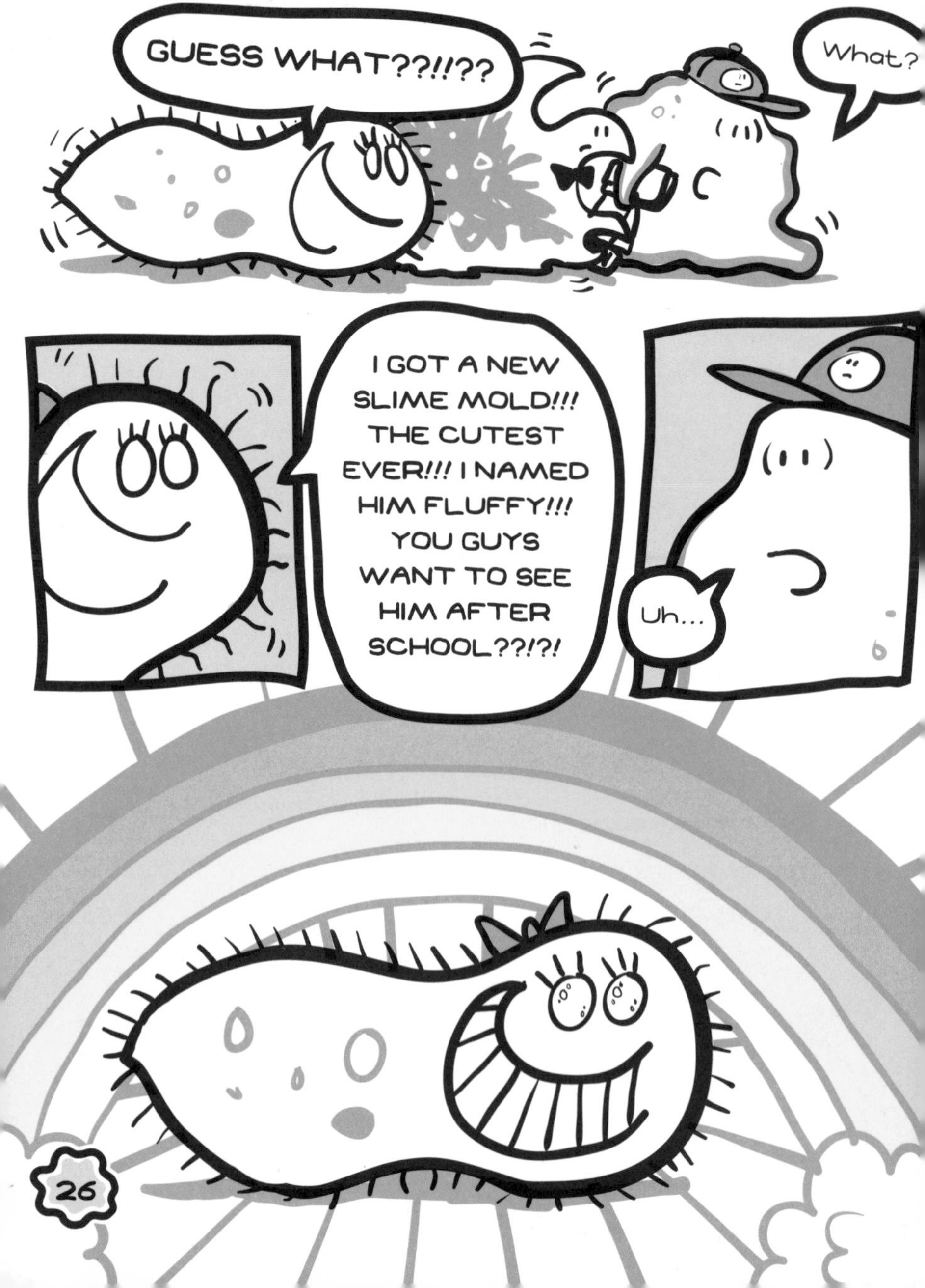
GUESS WHAT??!!??
What?
I GOT A NEW SLIME MOLD!!! THE CUTEST EVER!!! I NAMED HIM FLUFFY!!! YOU GUYS WANT TO SEE HIM AFTER SCHOOL??!?!
Uh...

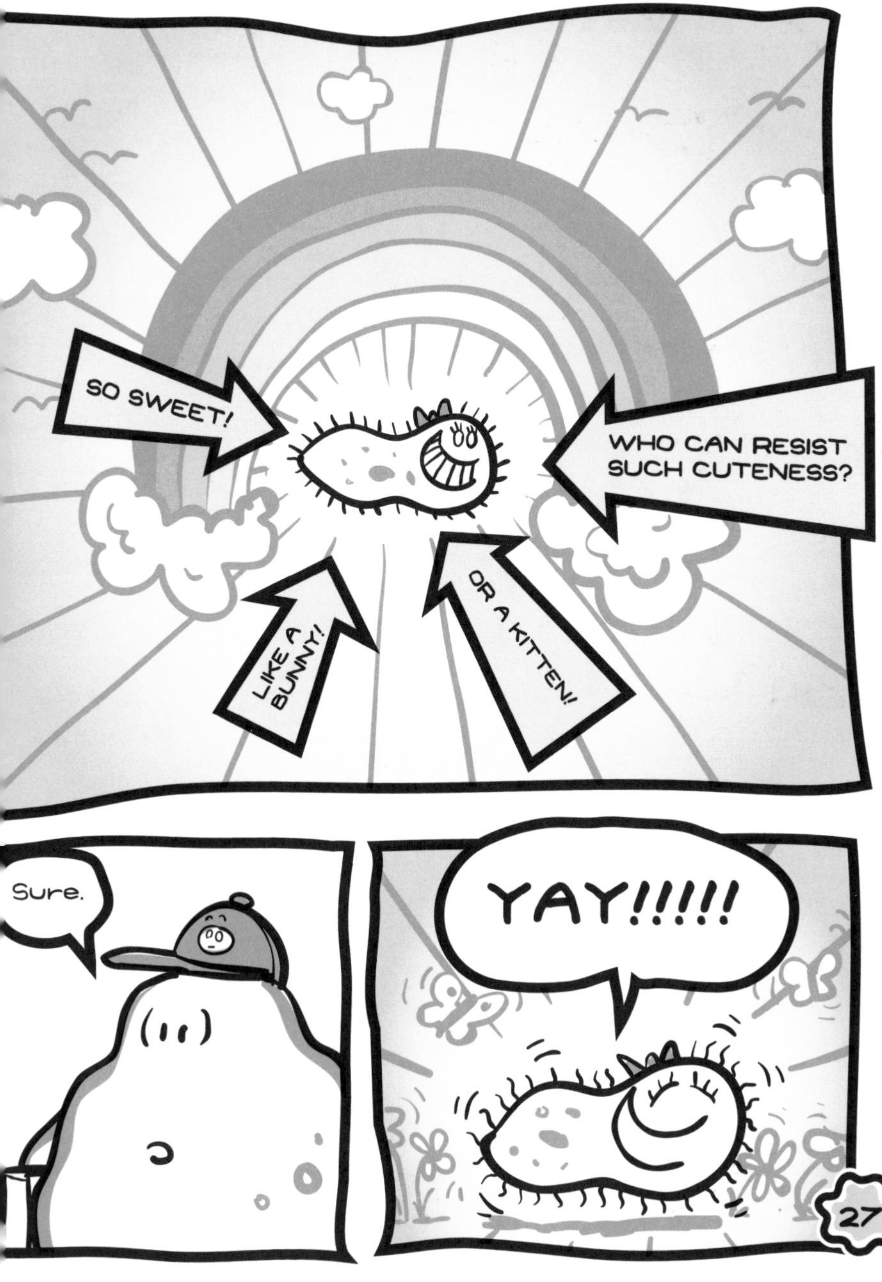
SO SWEET!
WHO CAN RESIST SUCH CUTENESS?
LIKE A BUNNY!
OR A KITTEN!
Sure.
YAY!!!!!

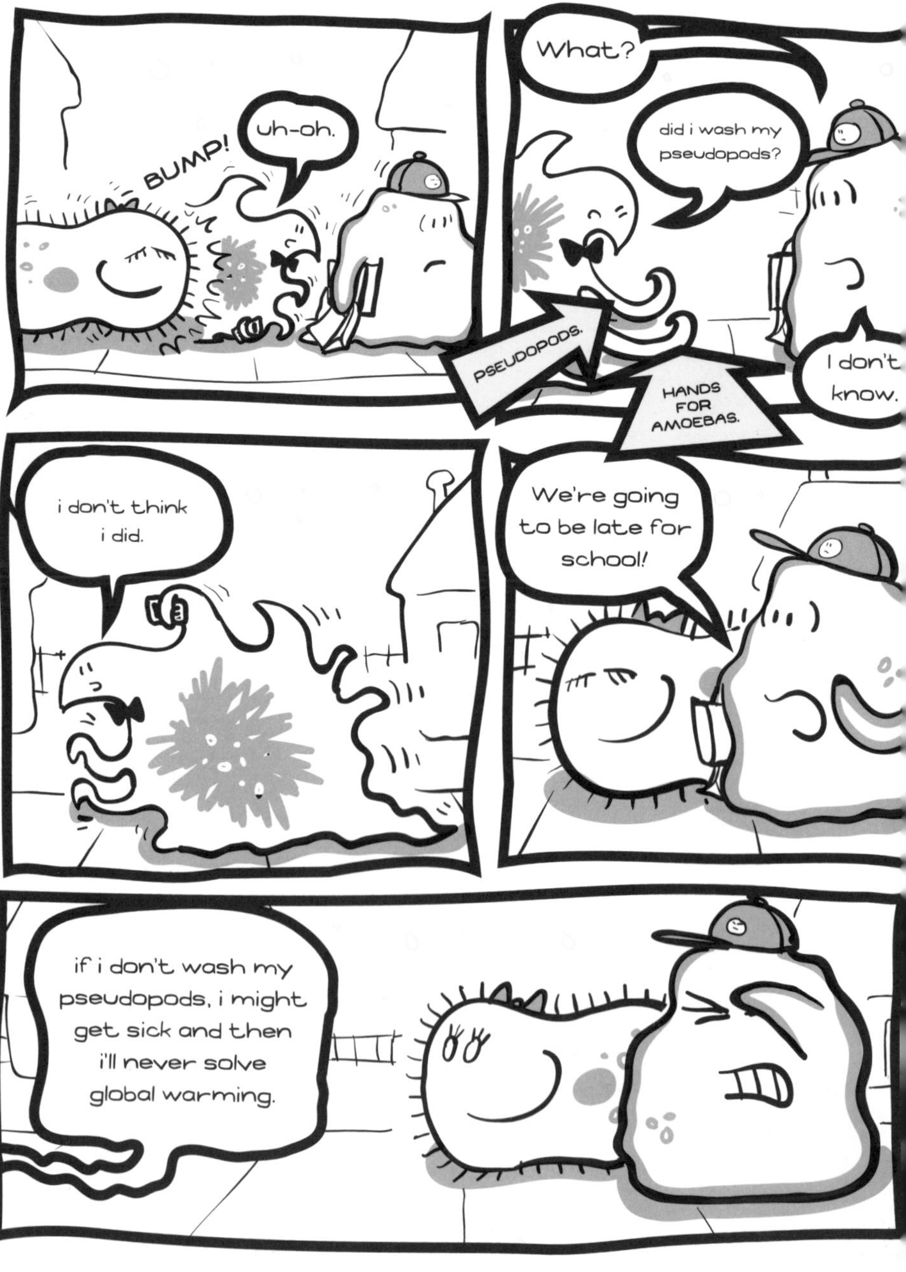
BUMP!
uh-oh.
What?
did i wash my pseudopods?
PSEUDOPODS.
HANDS FOR AMOEBAS.
I don't know.
i don't think i did.
We're going to be late for school!
if i don't wash my pseudopods, i might get sick and then i'll never solve global warming.

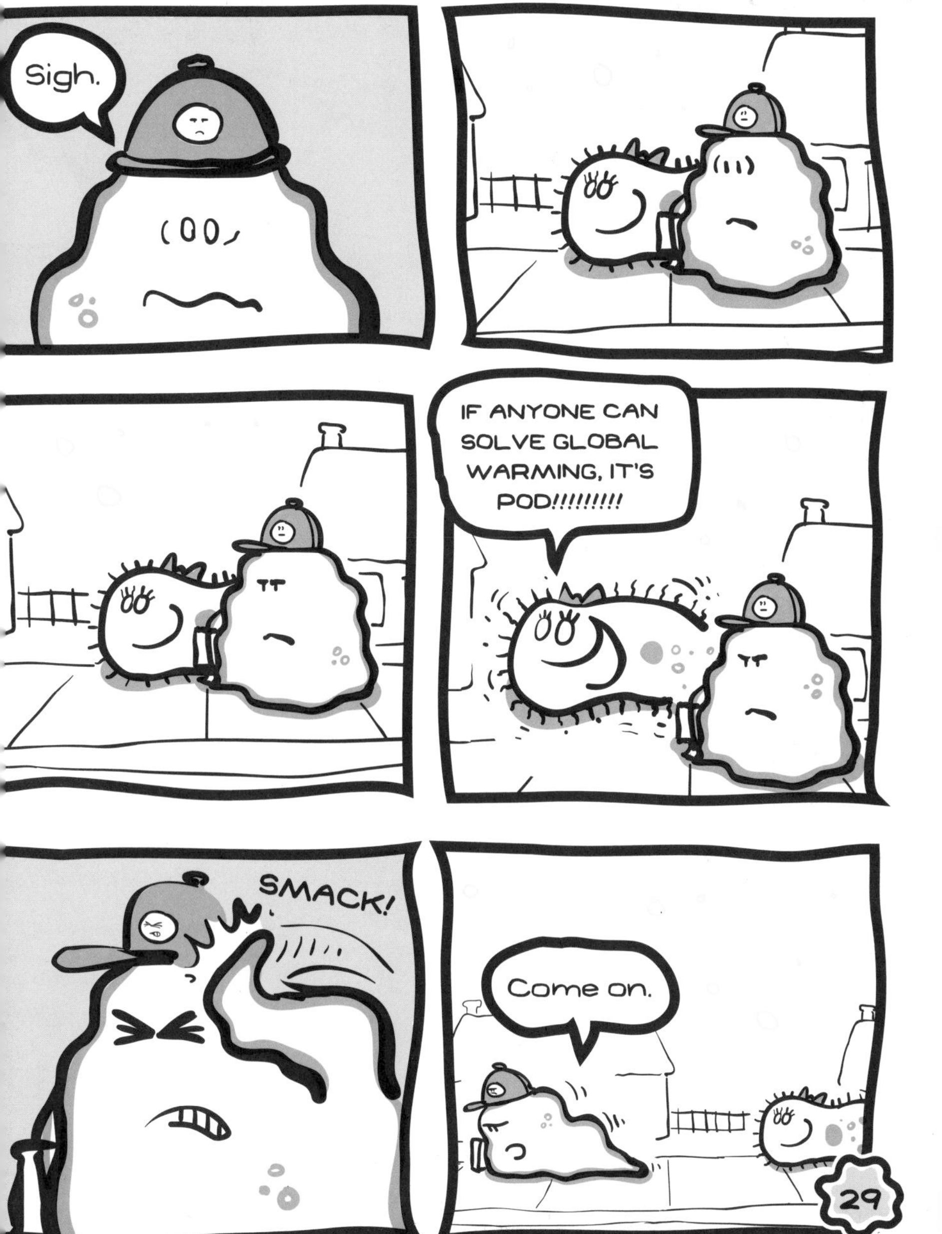
Sigh.
IF ANYONE CAN SOLVE GLOBAL WARMING, IT'S POD!!!!!!!!!
SMACK!
Come on.

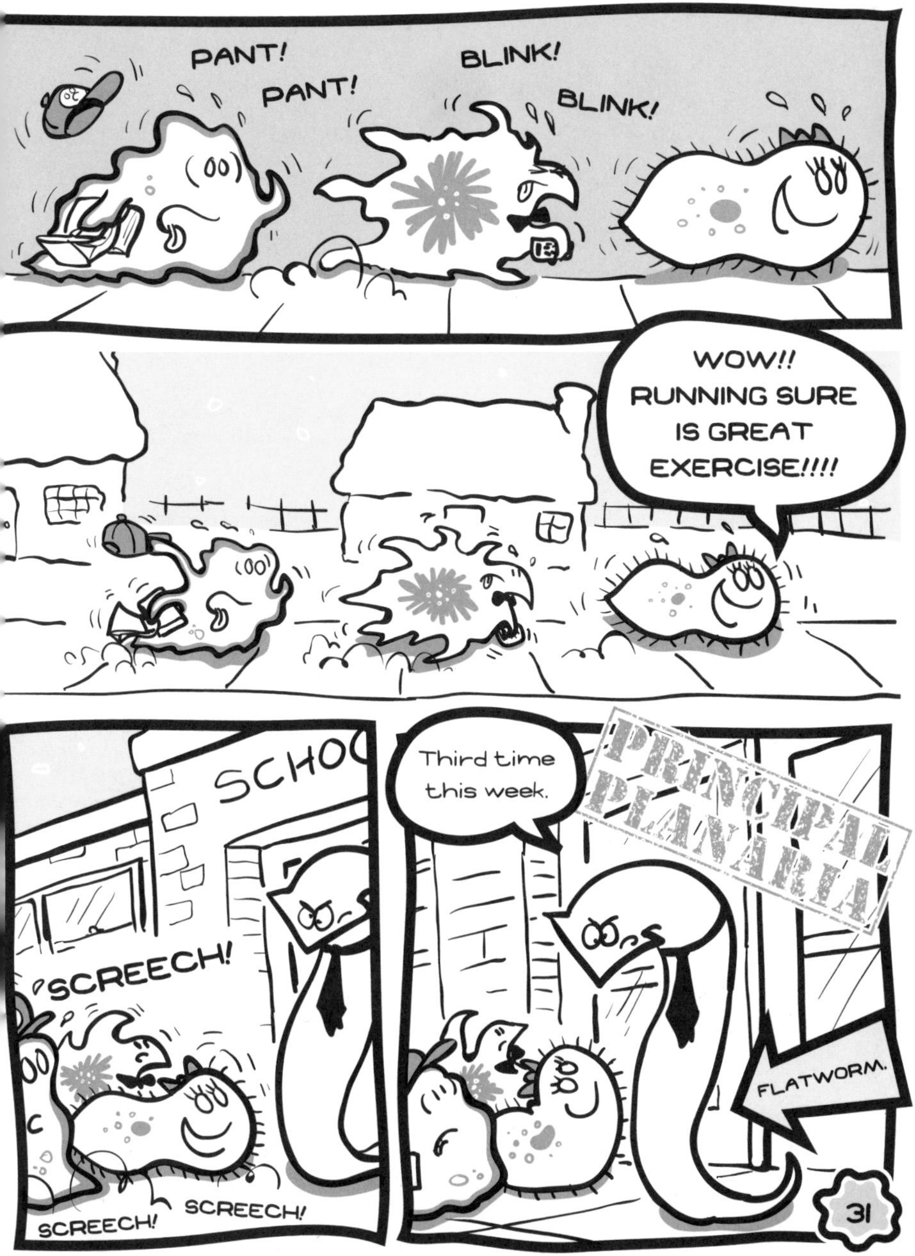

PANT!
PANT!
BLINK!
BLINK!
WOW!! RUNNING SURE IS GREAT EXERCISE!!!!
SCHO
SCREECH!
SCREECH!
SCREECH!
Third time this week.
PRINCIPAL PLANARIA
FLATWORM.

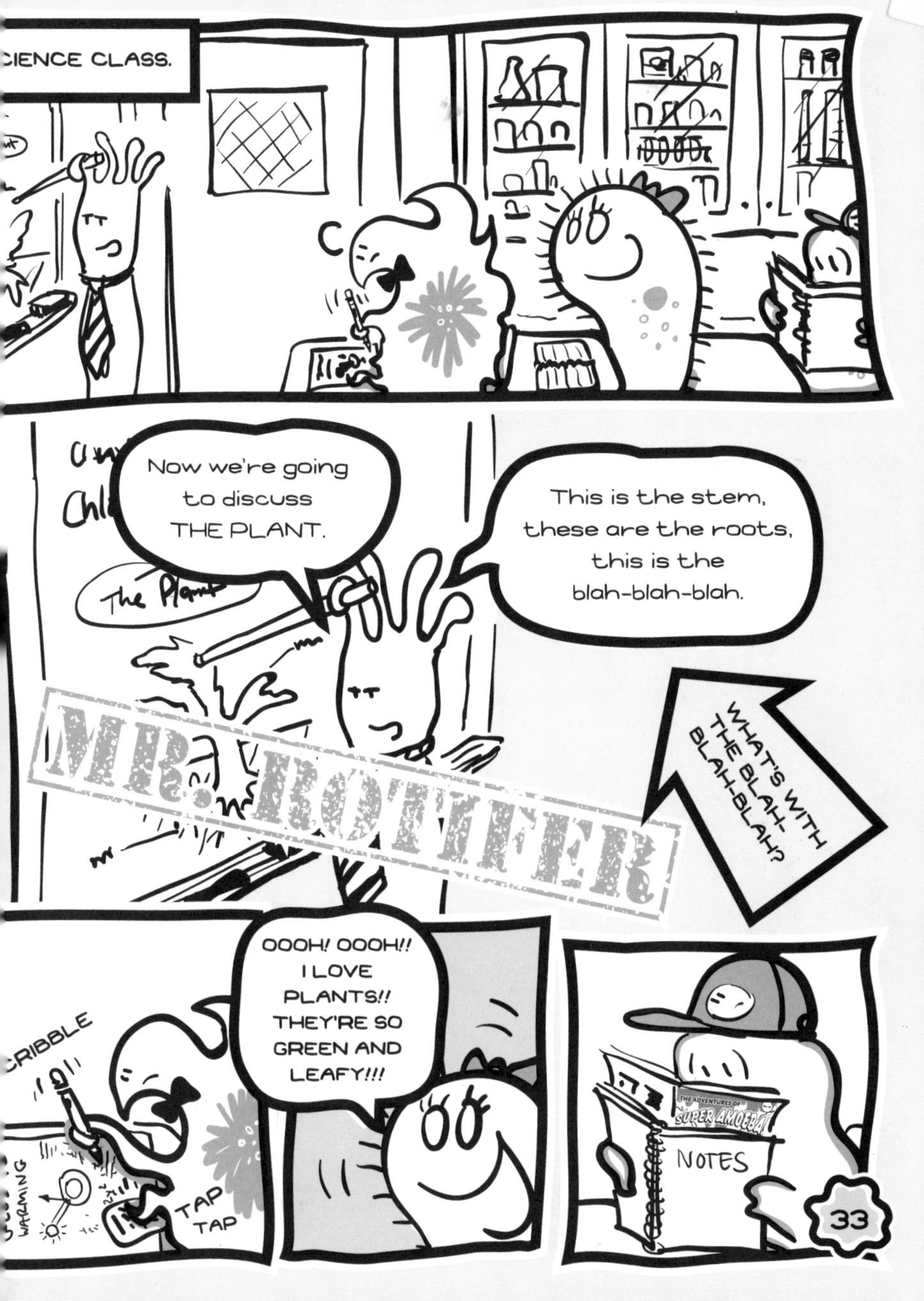
CIENCE CLASS.
Now we're going to discuss THE PLANT.
The Plant
This is the stem, these are the roots, this is the blah-blah-blah.
MR. ROTIFER
WHAT'S WITH THE BLAH-BLAH-BLAH?
CRIBBLE
TAP TAP
OOOH! OOOH!! I LOVE PLANTS!! THEY'RE SO GREEN AND LEAFY!!!
THE ADVENTURES OF SUPER AMOEBA!
NOTES

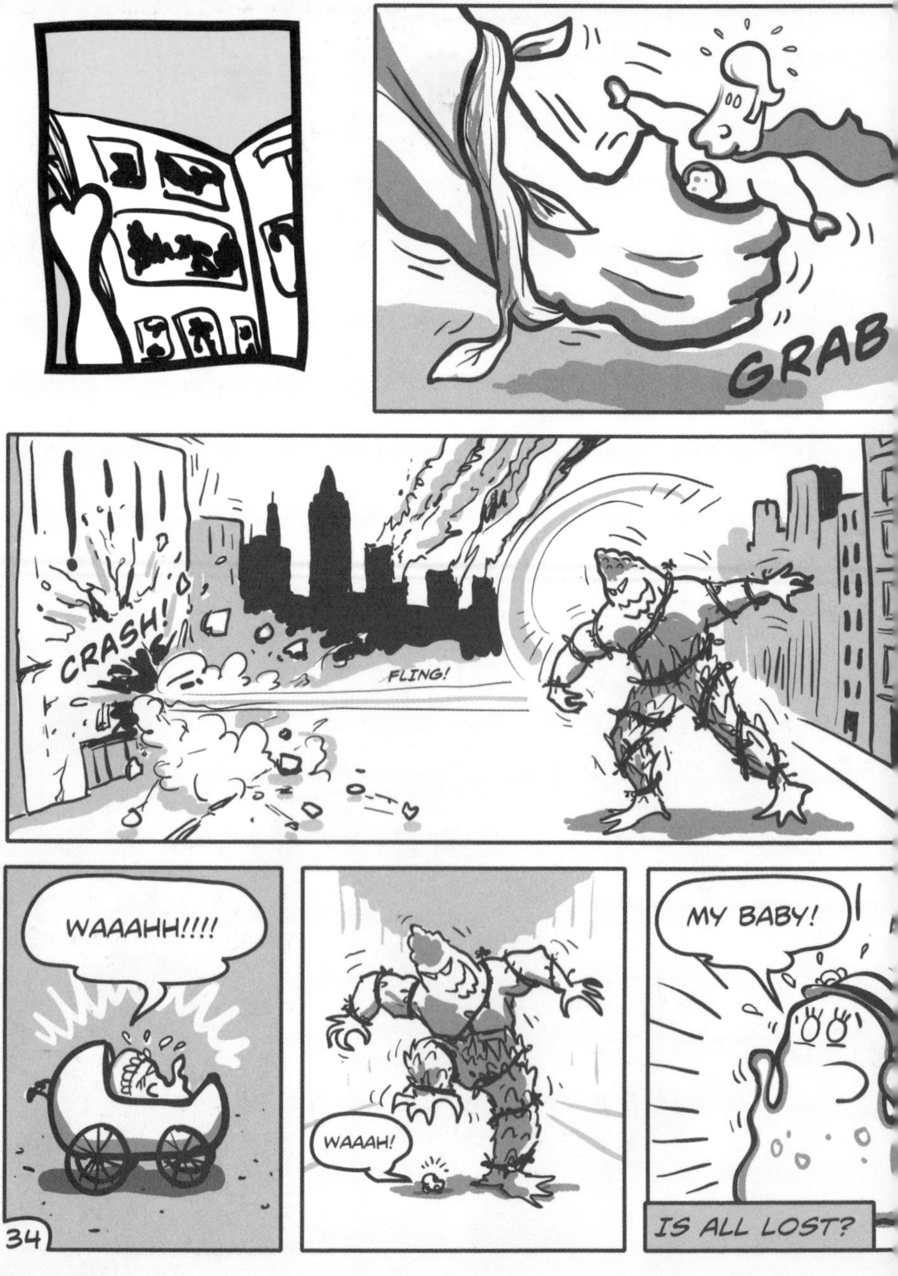
GRAB
CRASH!
FLING!
WAAAHH!!!!
WAAAH!
MY BABY!
IS ALL LOST?

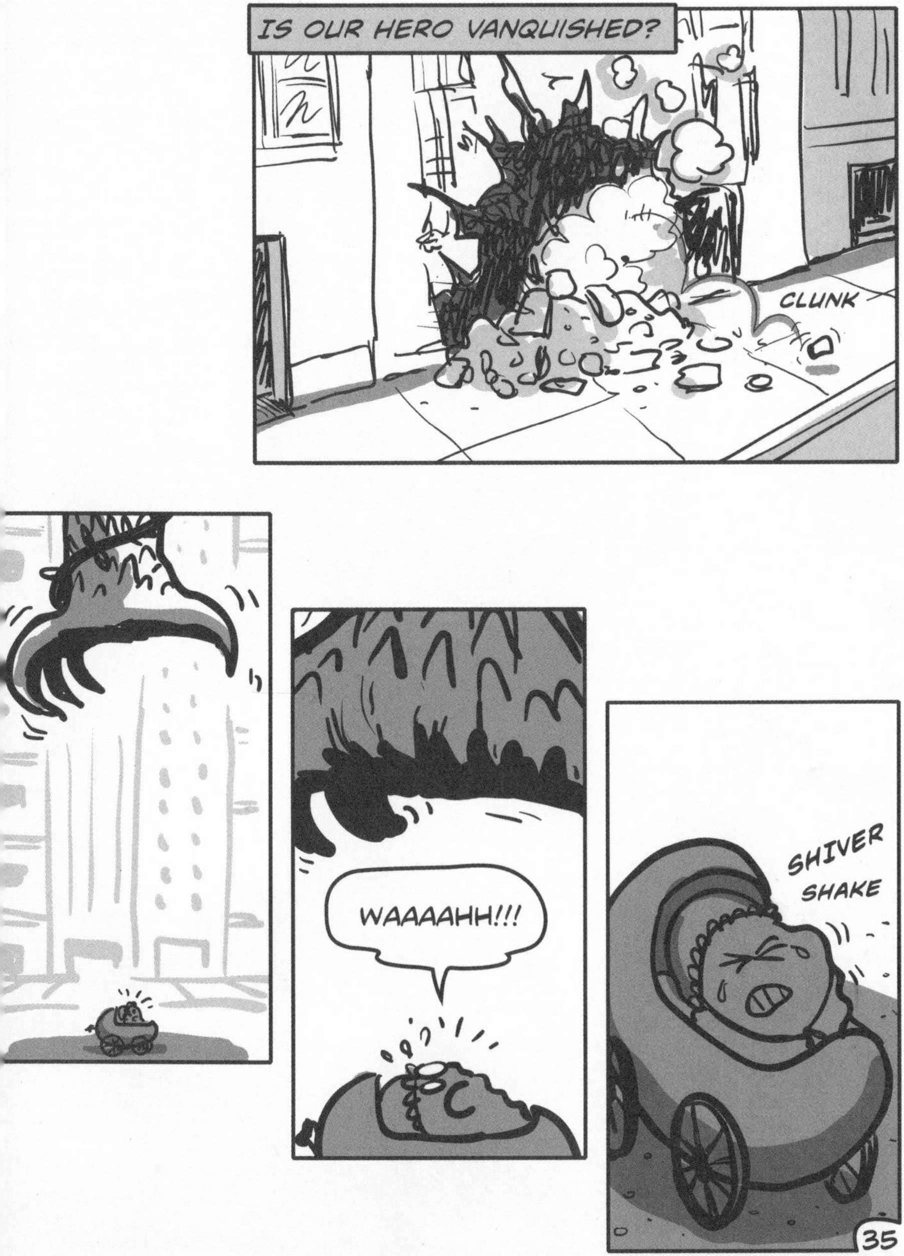
IS OUR HERO VANQUISHED?
CLUNK
WAAAAHH!!!
SHIVER
SHAKE

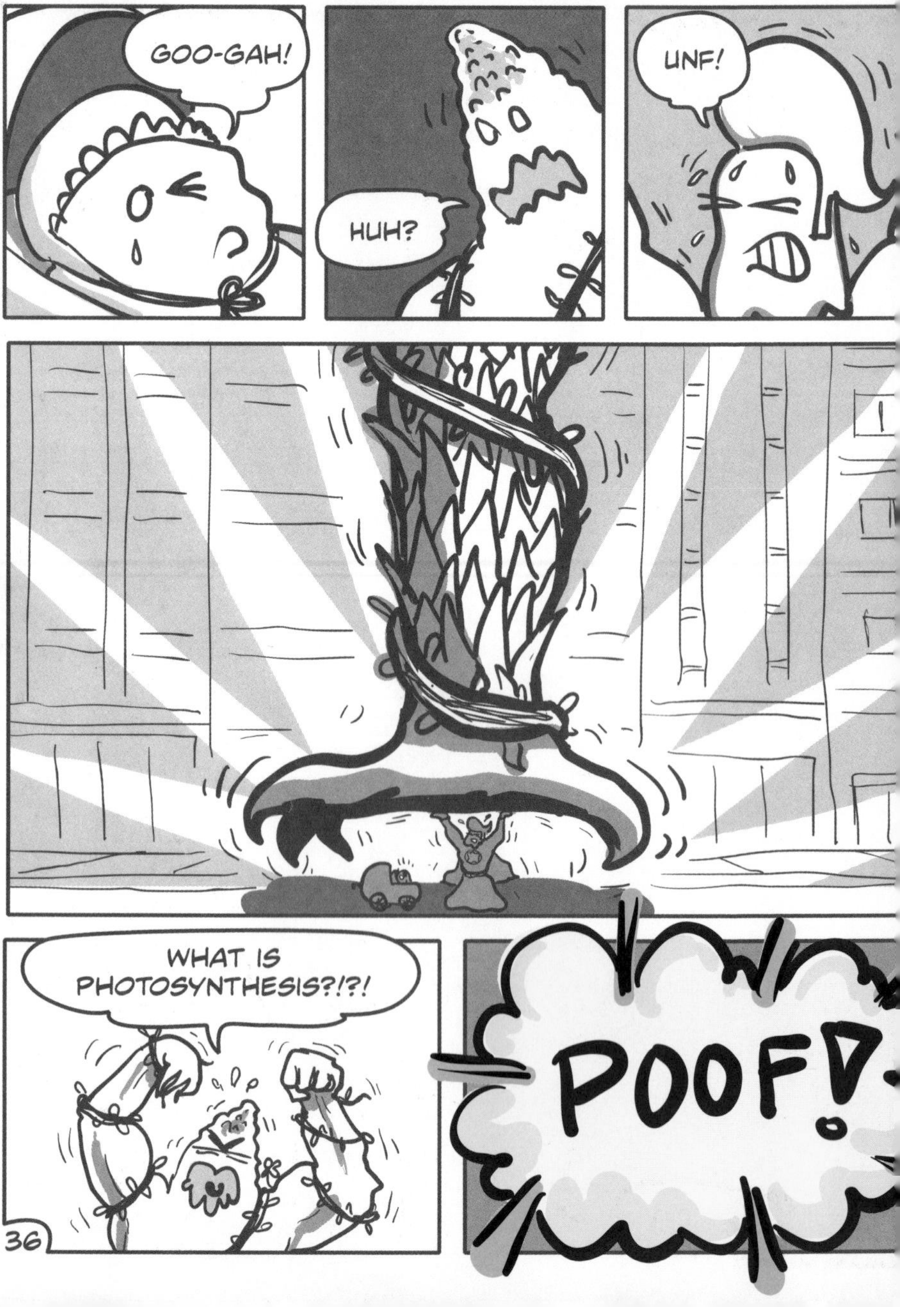
GOO-GAH!
HUH?
UNF!
WHAT IS PHOTOSYNTHESIS?!?!
POOF!

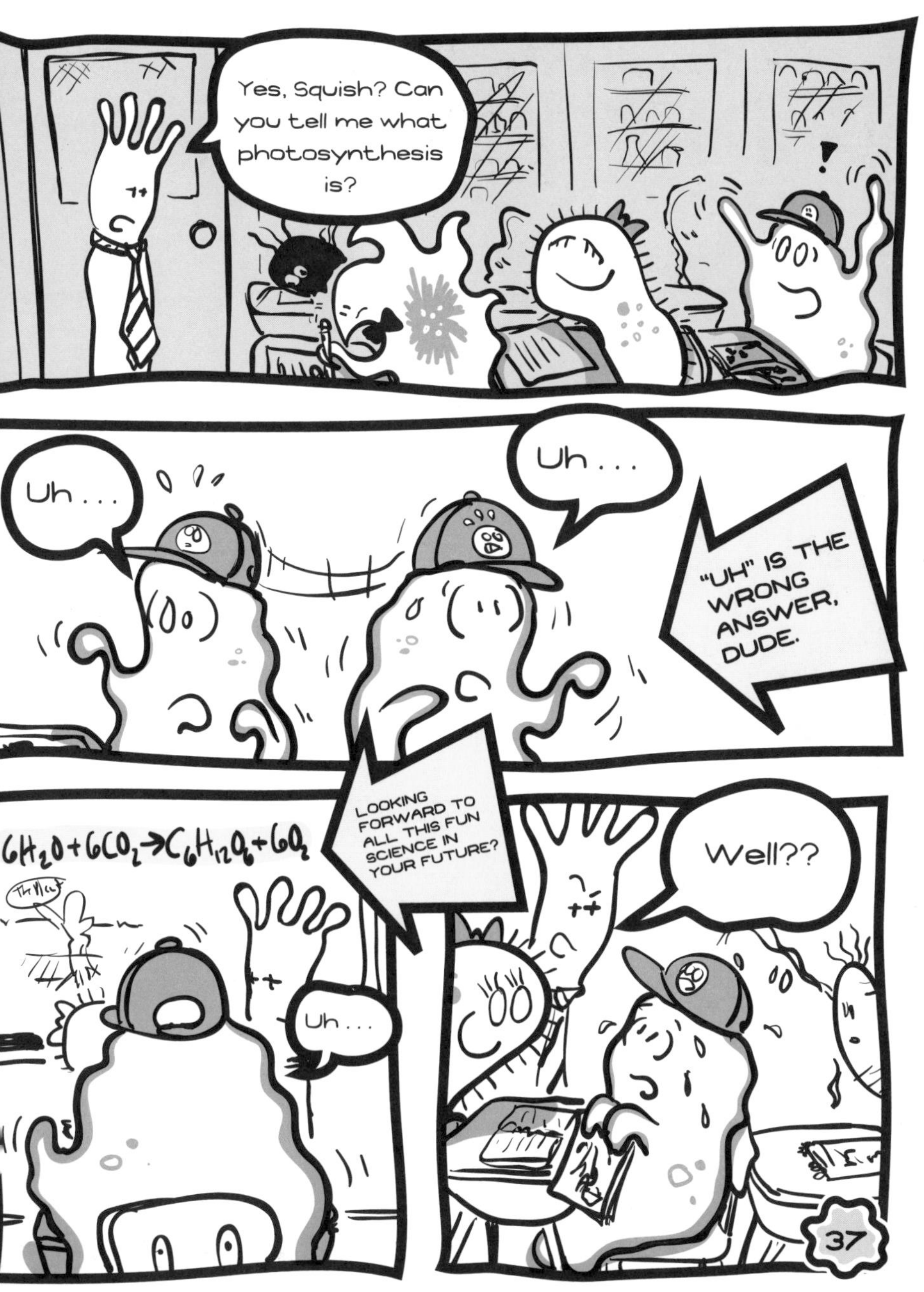

Yes, Squish? Can you tell me what photosynthesis is?
Uh . . .
Uh . . .
"UH" IS THE WRONG ANSWER, DUDE.
$6H_2O + 6CO_2 \rightarrow C_6H_{12}O_6 + 6O_2$
LOOKING FORWARD TO ALL THIS FUN SCIENCE IN YOUR FUTURE?
Uh . . .
Well??

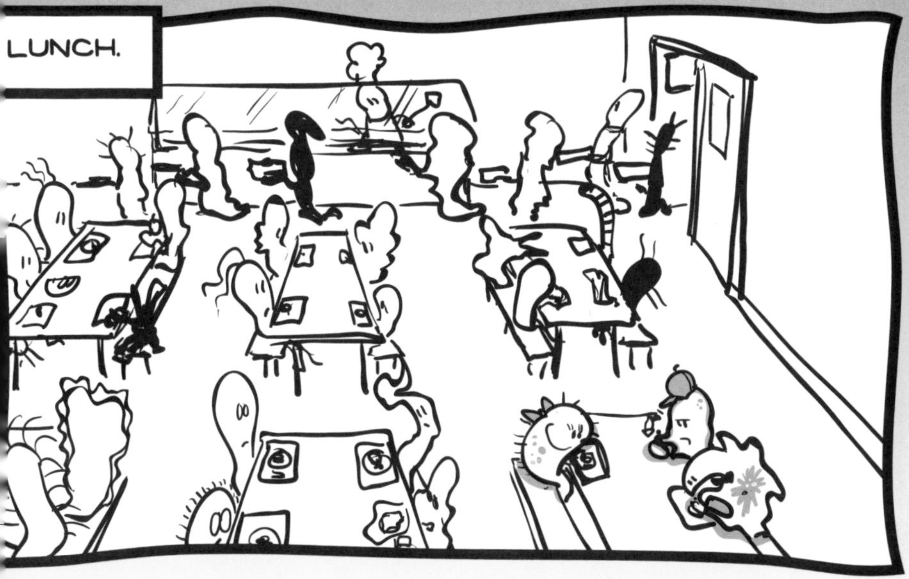
LUNCH.

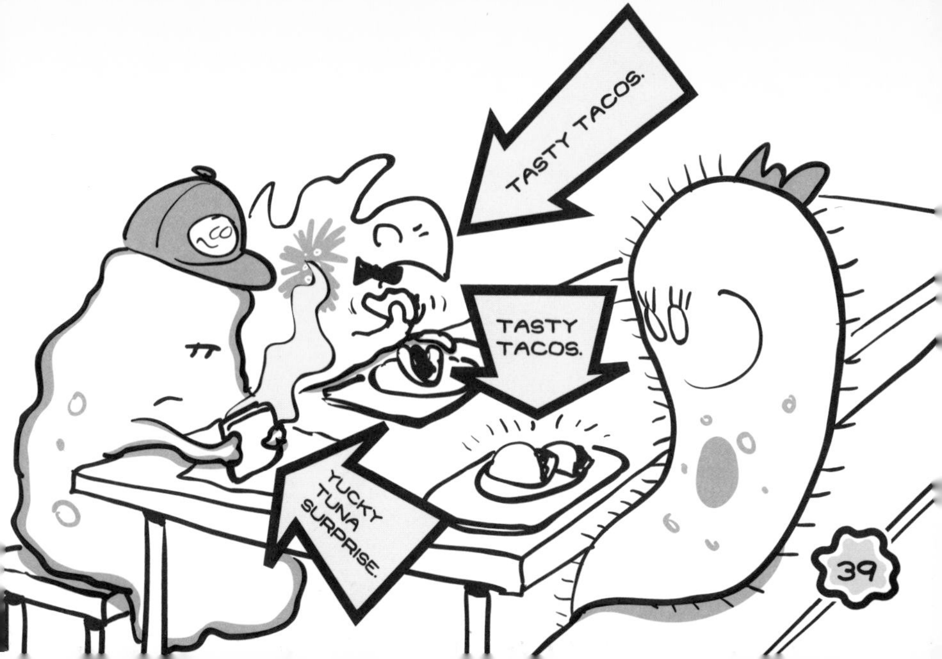
TASTY TACOS.
TASTY TACOS.
YUCKY TUNA SURPRISE.

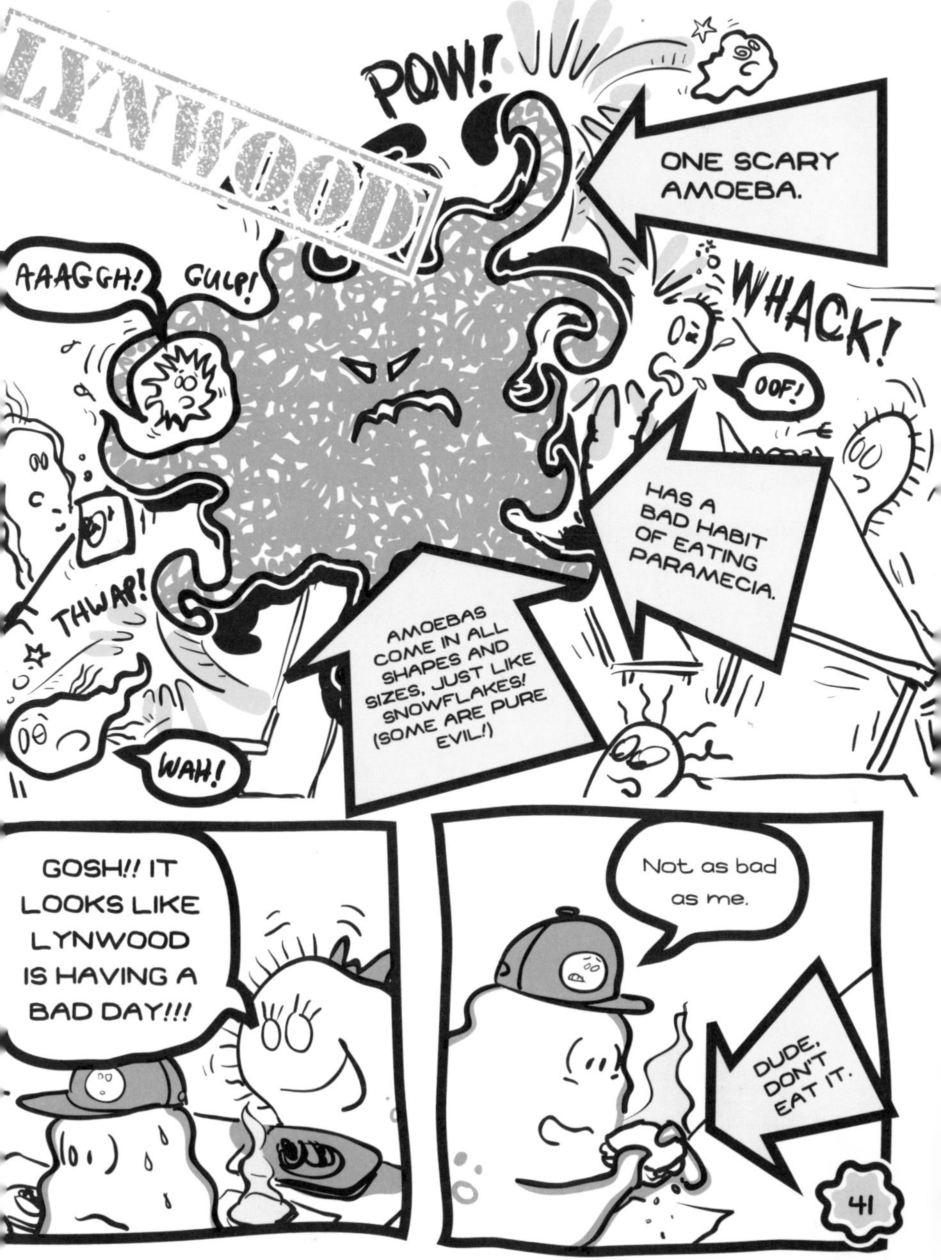

LYNWOOD
POW!
ONE SCARY AMOEBA.
AAAGGH!
GULP!
WHACK!
OOF!
HAS A BAD HABIT OF EATING PARAMECIA.
THWAP!
AMOEBAS COME IN ALL SHAPES AND SIZES, JUST LIKE SNOWFLAKES! (SOME ARE PURE EVIL!)
WAH!
GOSH!! IT LOOKS LIKE LYNWOOD IS HAVING A BAD DAY!!!
Not as bad as me.
DUDE, DON'T EAT IT.

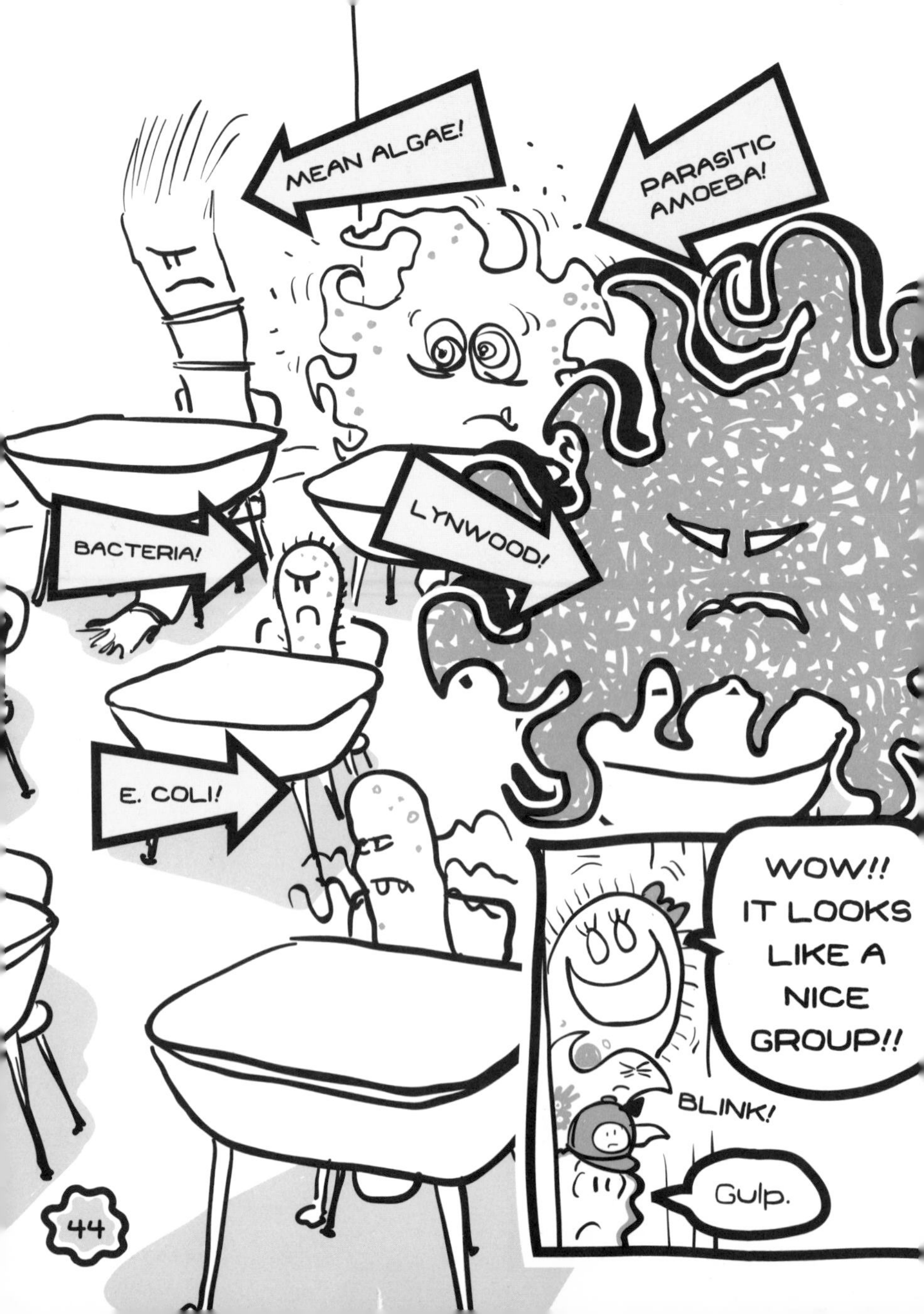
MEAN ALGAE!
PARASITIC AMOEBA!
BACTERIA!
LYNWOOD!
E. COLI!
WOW!! IT LOOKS LIKE A NICE GROUP!!
BLINK!
Gulp.

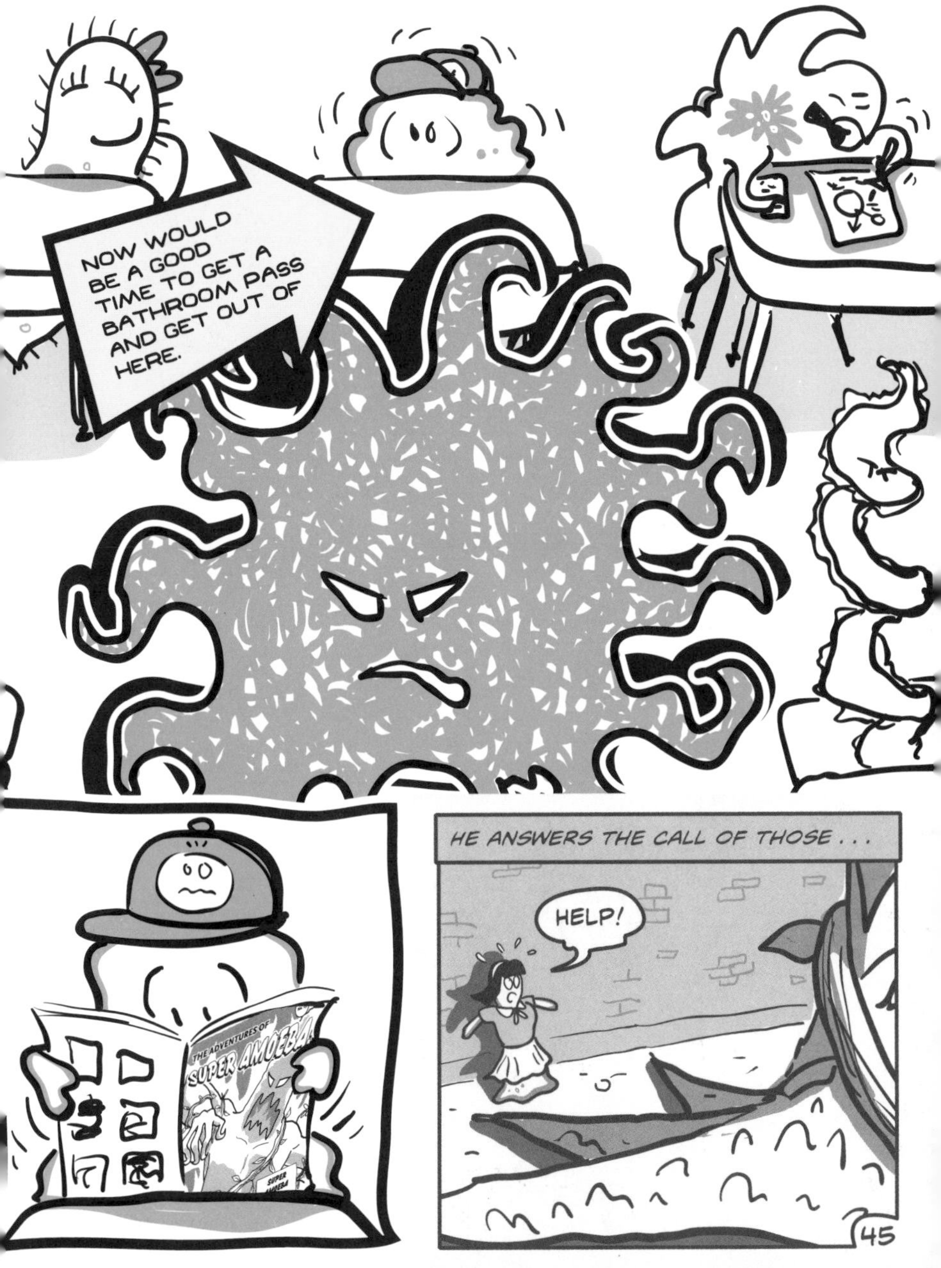
NOW WOULD BE A GOOD TIME TO GET A BATHROOM PASS AND GET OUT OF HERE.
THE ADVENTURES OF SUPER AMOEBA
HE ANSWERS THE CALL OF THOSE . . .
HELP!

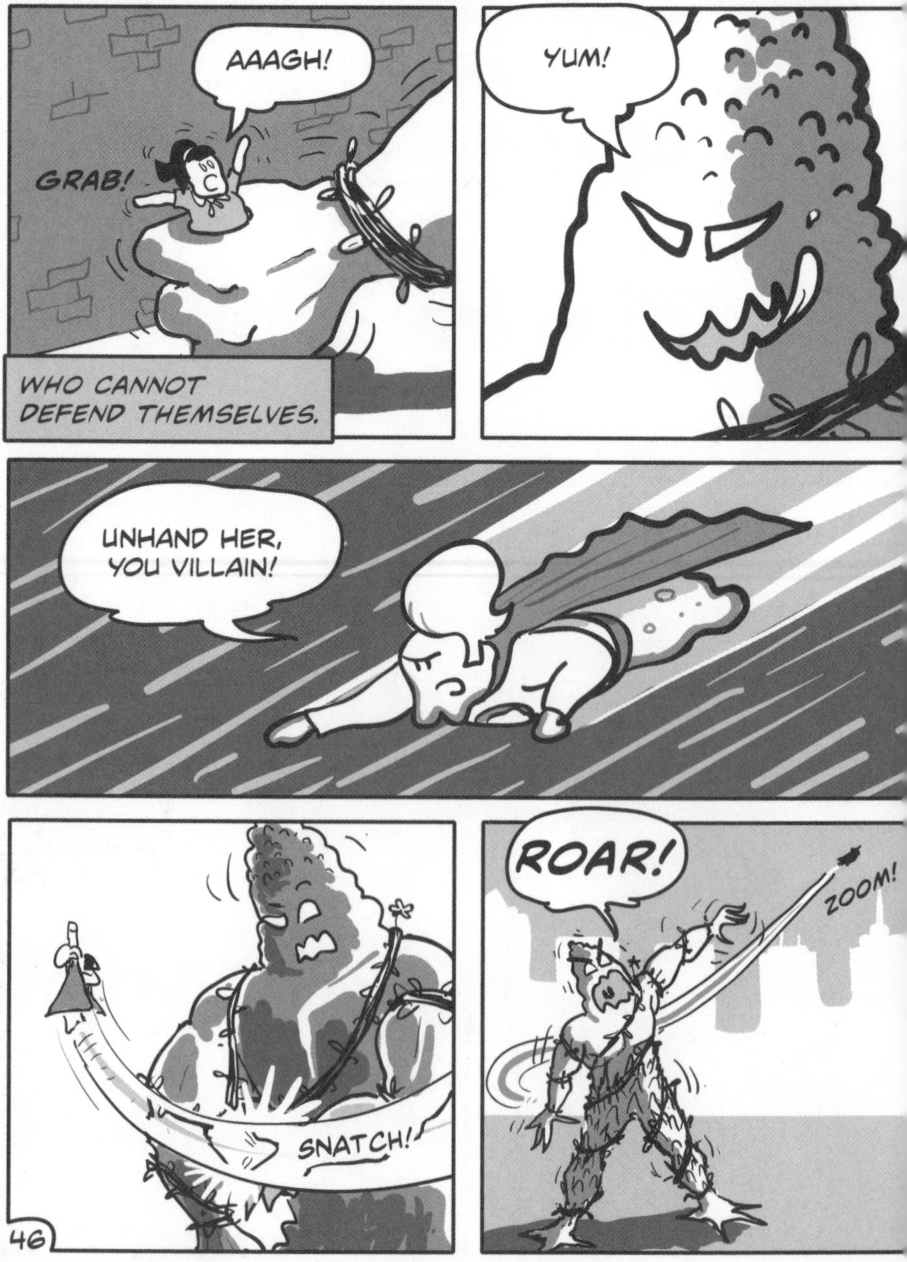
AAAGH!
GRAB!
WHO CANNOT DEFEND THEMSELVES.
YUM!
UNHAND HER, YOU VILLAIN!
SNATCH!
ROAR!
ZOOM!

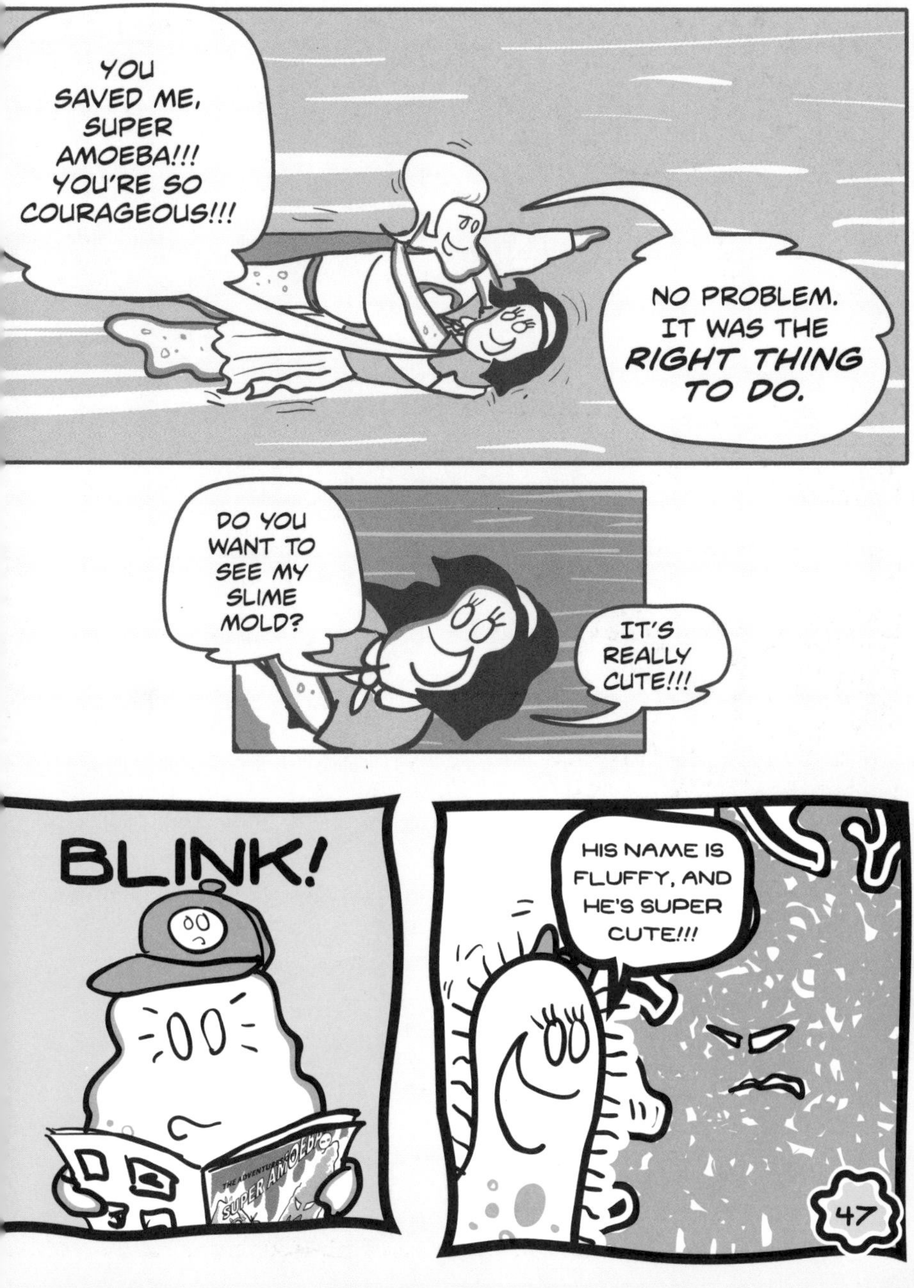
YOU SAVED ME, SUPER AMOEBA!!! YOU'RE SO COURAGEOUS!!!
NO PROBLEM. IT WAS THE *RIGHT THING TO DO.*
DO YOU WANT TO SEE MY SLIME MOLD?
IT'S REALLY CUTE!!!
BLINK!
THE ADVENTURES OF SUPER AMOEBA
HIS NAME IS FLUFFY, AND HE'S SUPER CUTE!!!

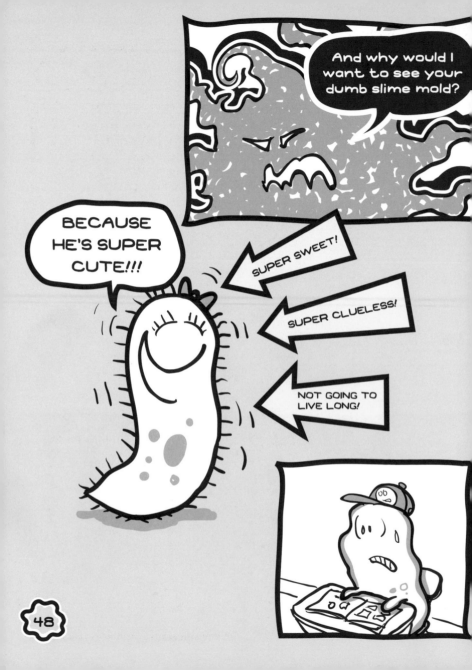

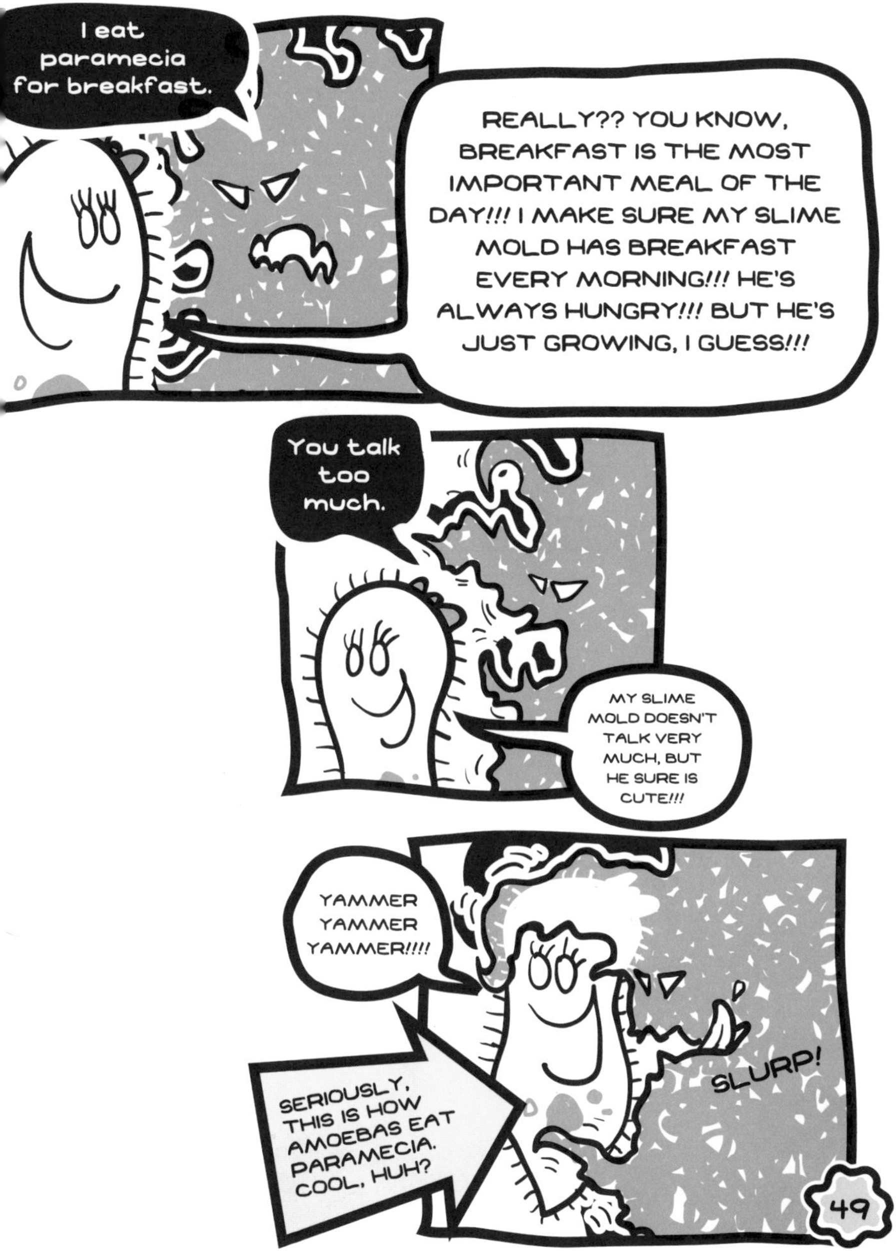

I eat paramecia for breakfast.
REALLY?? YOU KNOW, BREAKFAST IS THE MOST IMPORTANT MEAL OF THE DAY!!! I MAKE SURE MY SLIME MOLD HAS BREAKFAST EVERY MORNING!!! HE'S ALWAYS HUNGRY!!! BUT HE'S JUST GROWING, I GUESS!!!
You talk too much.
MY SLIME MOLD DOESN'T TALK VERY MUCH, BUT HE SURE IS CUTE!!!
YAMMER YAMMER YAMMER!!!!
SERIOUSLY, THIS IS HOW AMOEBAS EAT PARAMECIA. COOL, HUH?
SLURP!

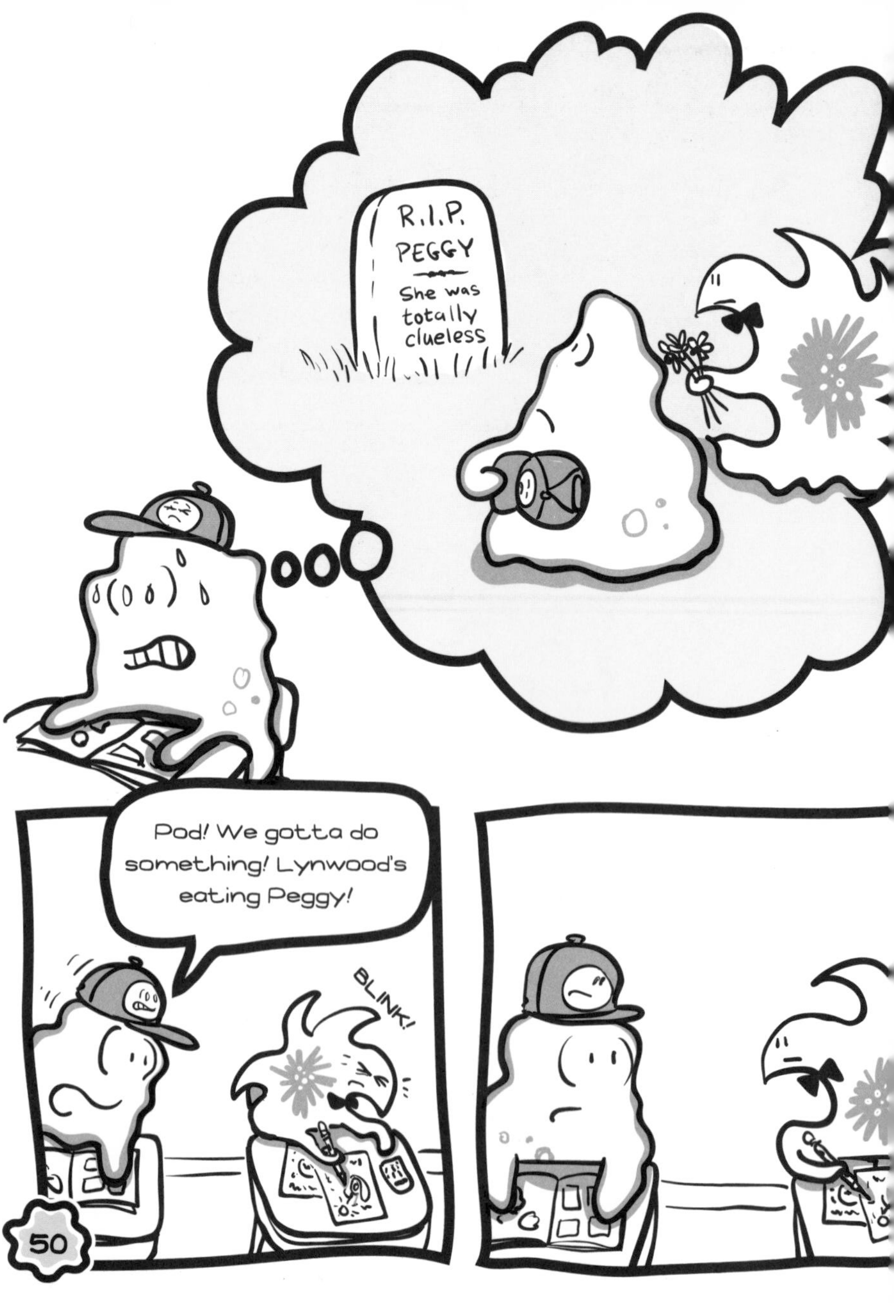
R.I.P.
PEGGY
She was totally clueless
Pod! We gotta do something! Lynwood's eating Peggy!
BLINK!

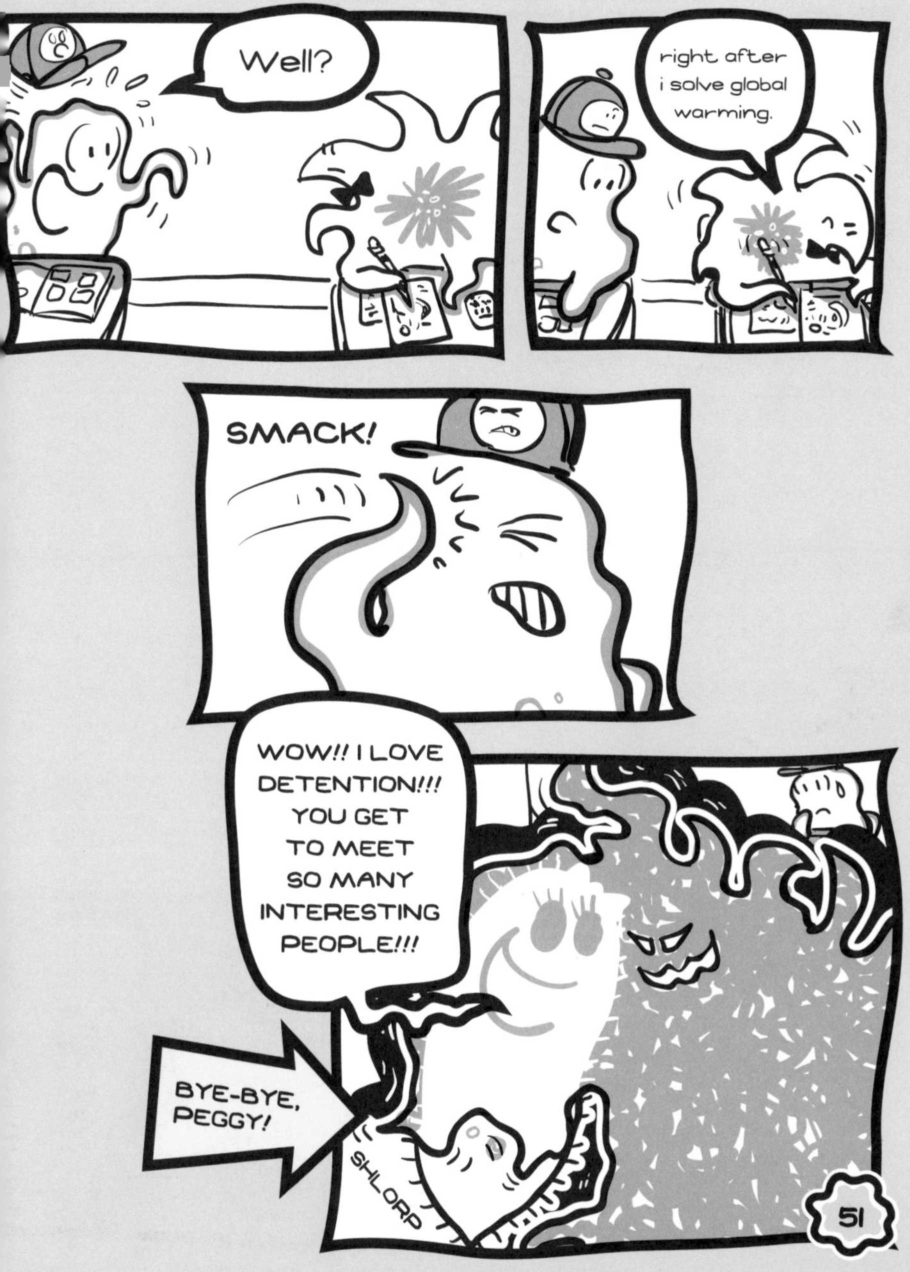
Well?
right after i solve global warming.
SMACK!
WOW!! I LOVE DETENTION!!! YOU GET TO MEET SO MANY INTERESTING PEOPLE!!!
BYE-BYE, PEGGY!
SHLORP

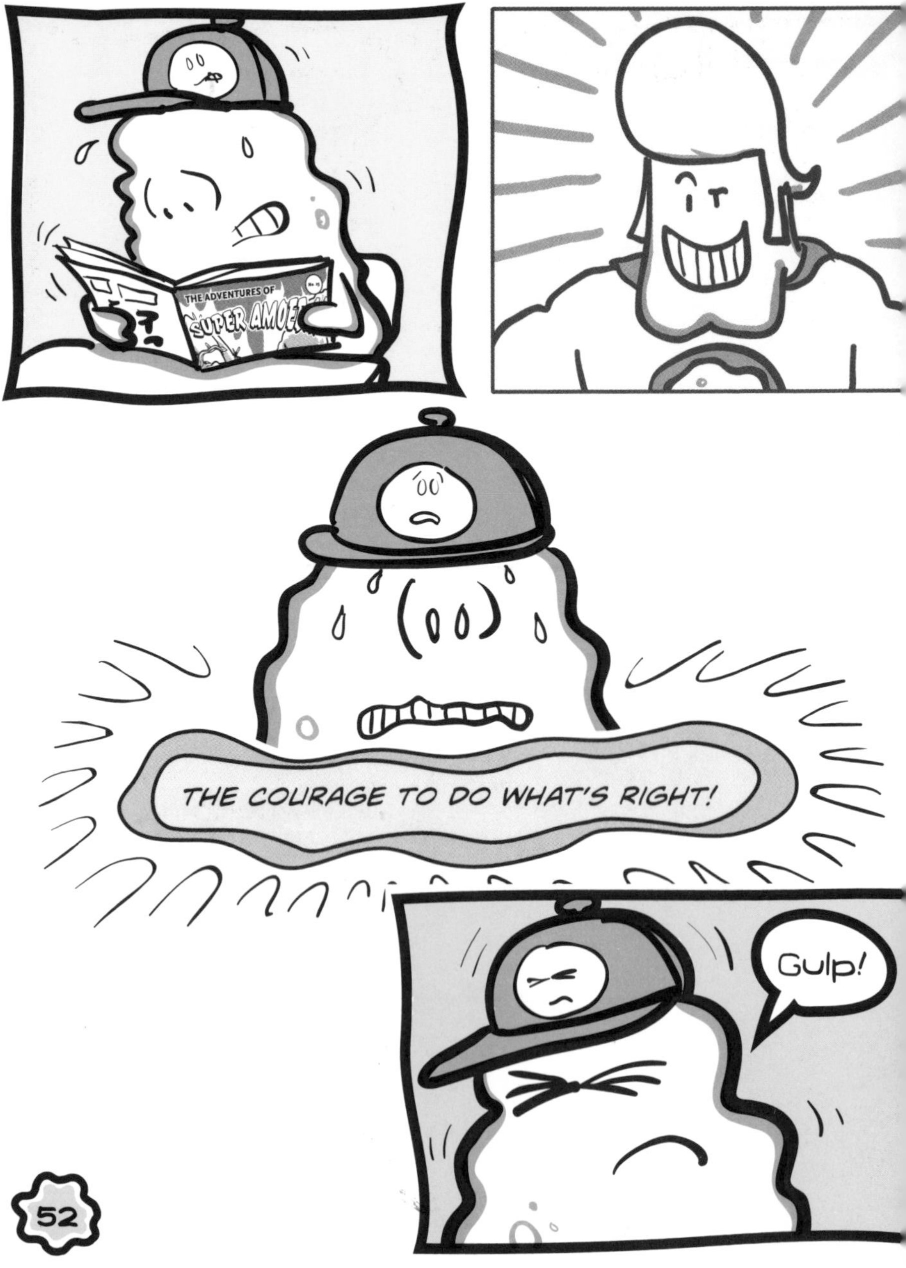
THE ADVENTURES OF
THE COURAGE TO DO WHAT'S RIGHT!
Gulp!

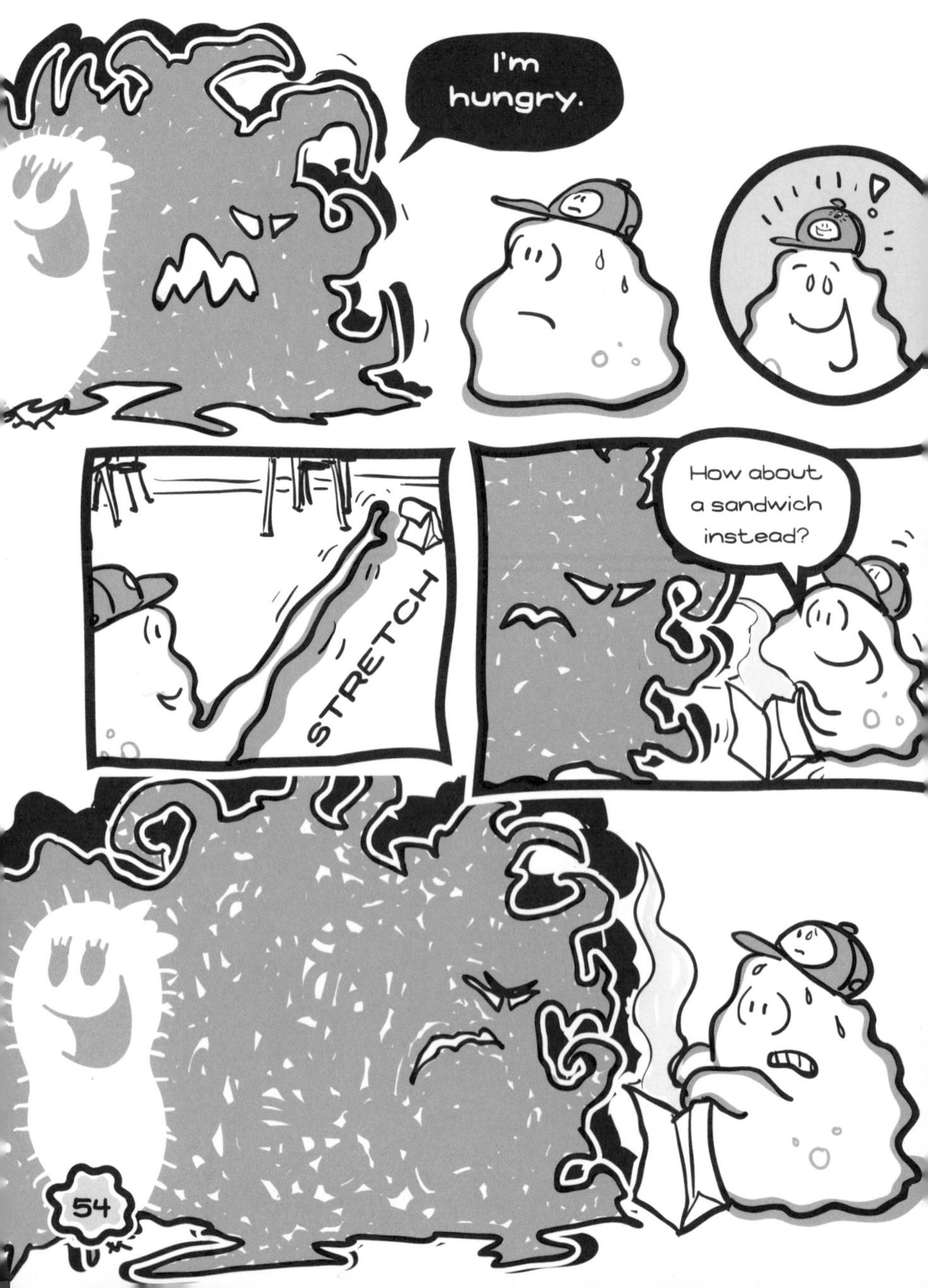
I'm hungry.
STRETCH
How about a sandwich instead?

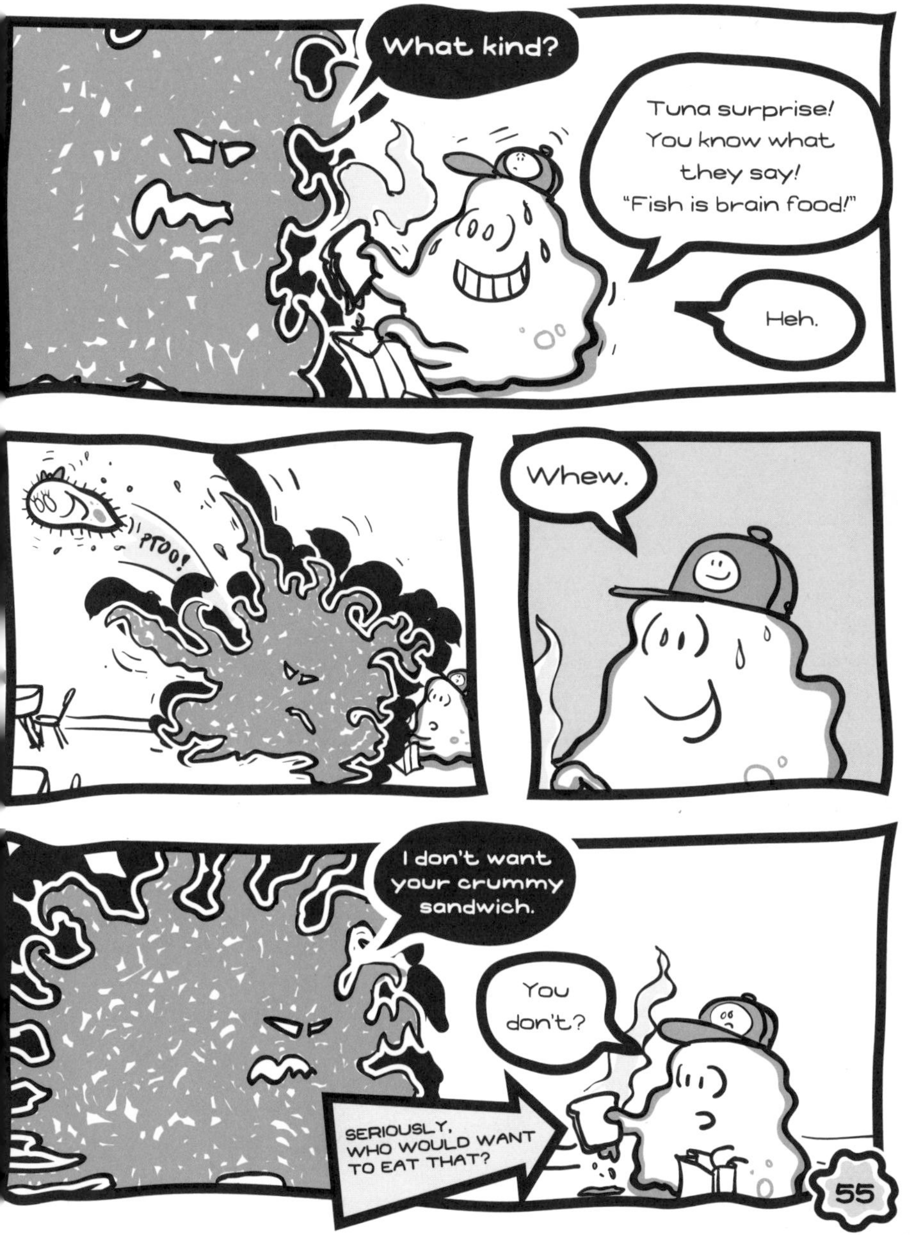
What kind?
Tuna surprise! You know what they say! "Fish is brain food!"
Heh.
PTOO!
Whew.
I don't want your crummy sandwich.
You don't?
SERIOUSLY, WHO WOULD WANT TO EAT THAT?

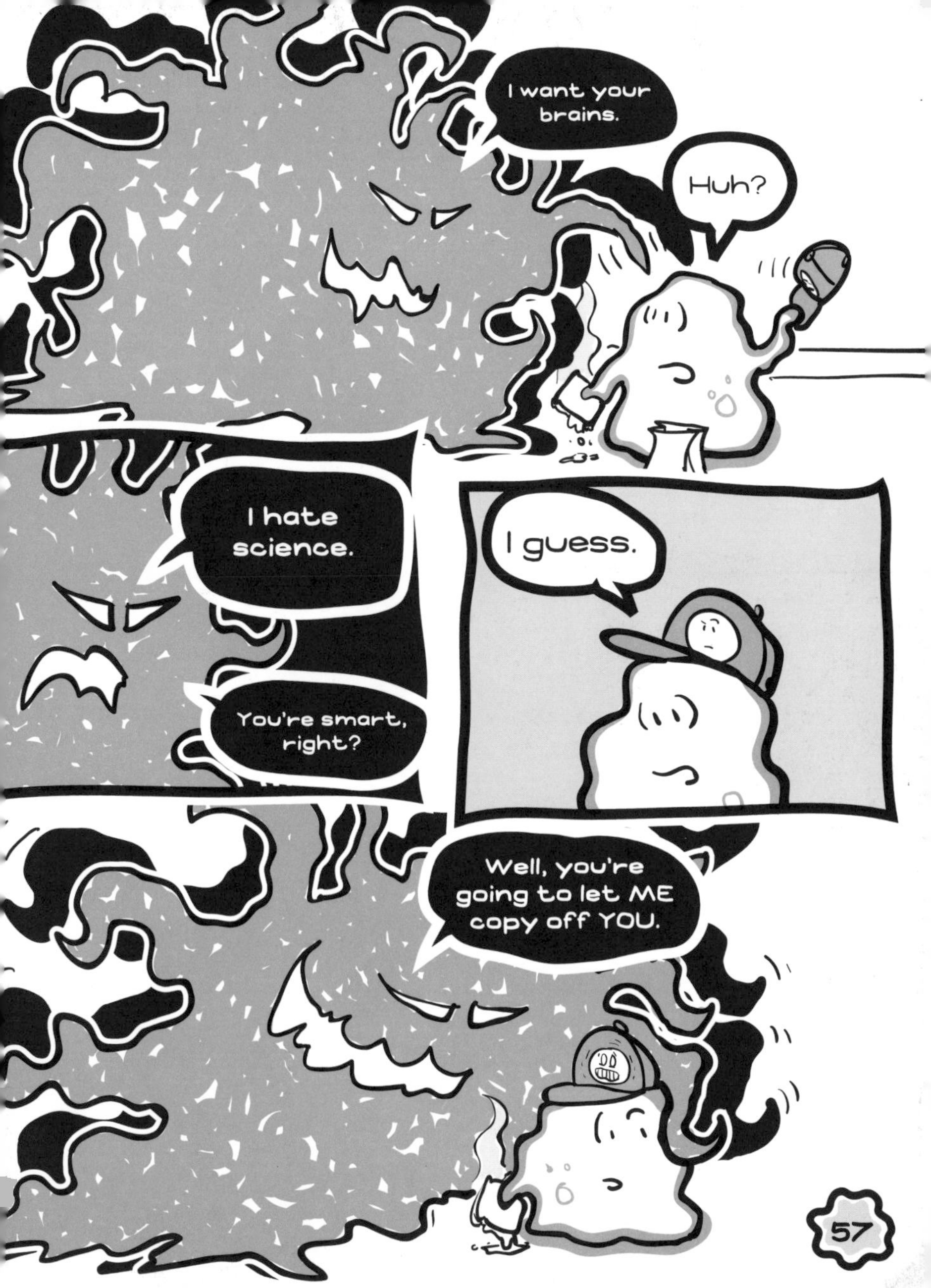
I want your brains.
Huh?
I hate science.
You're smart, right?
I guess.
Well, you're going to let ME copy off YOU.

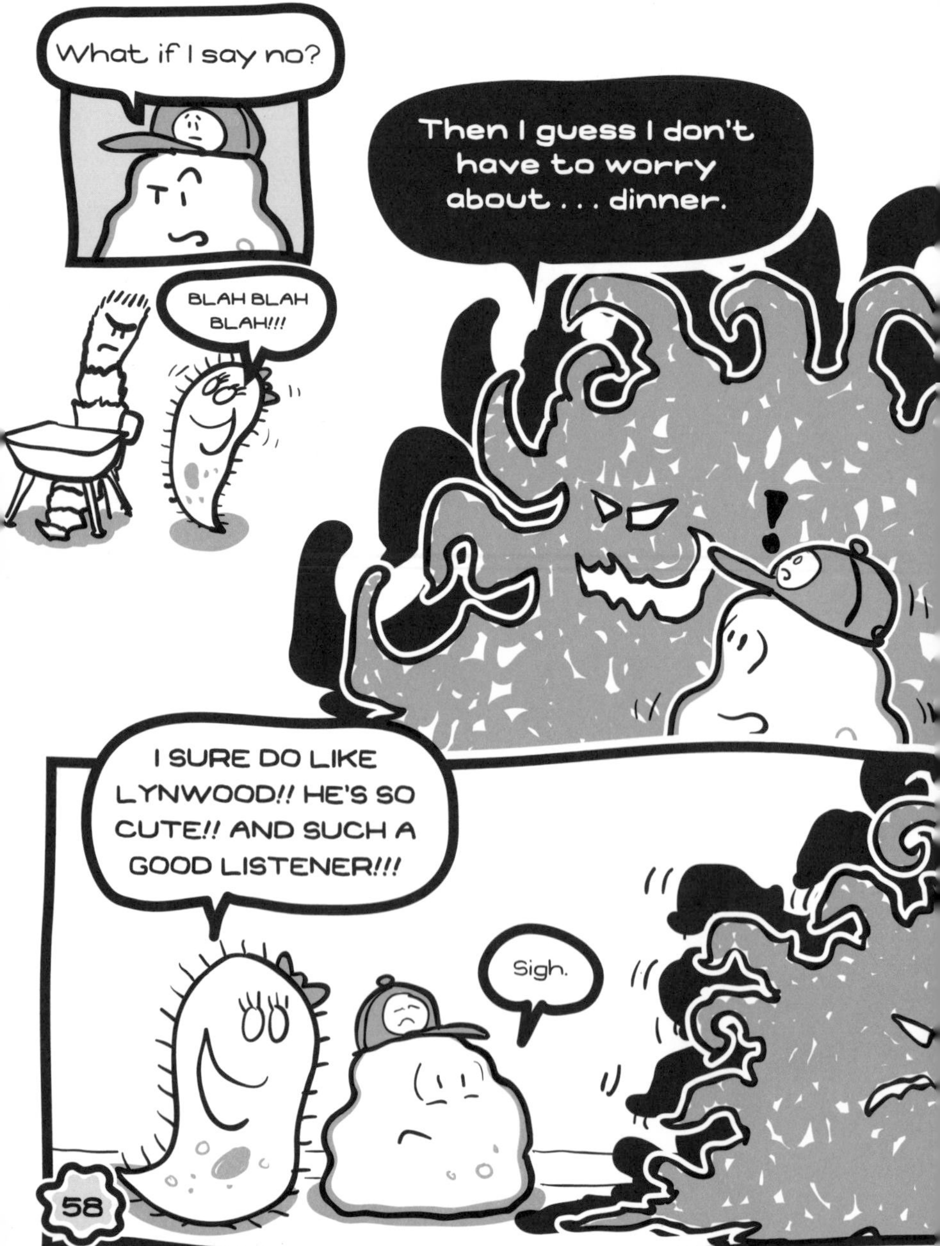

What if I say no?
Then I guess I don't have to worry about . . . dinner.
BLAH BLAH BLAH!!!
I SURE DO LIKE LYNWOOD!! HE'S SO CUTE!! AND SUCH A GOOD LISTENER!!!
Sigh.

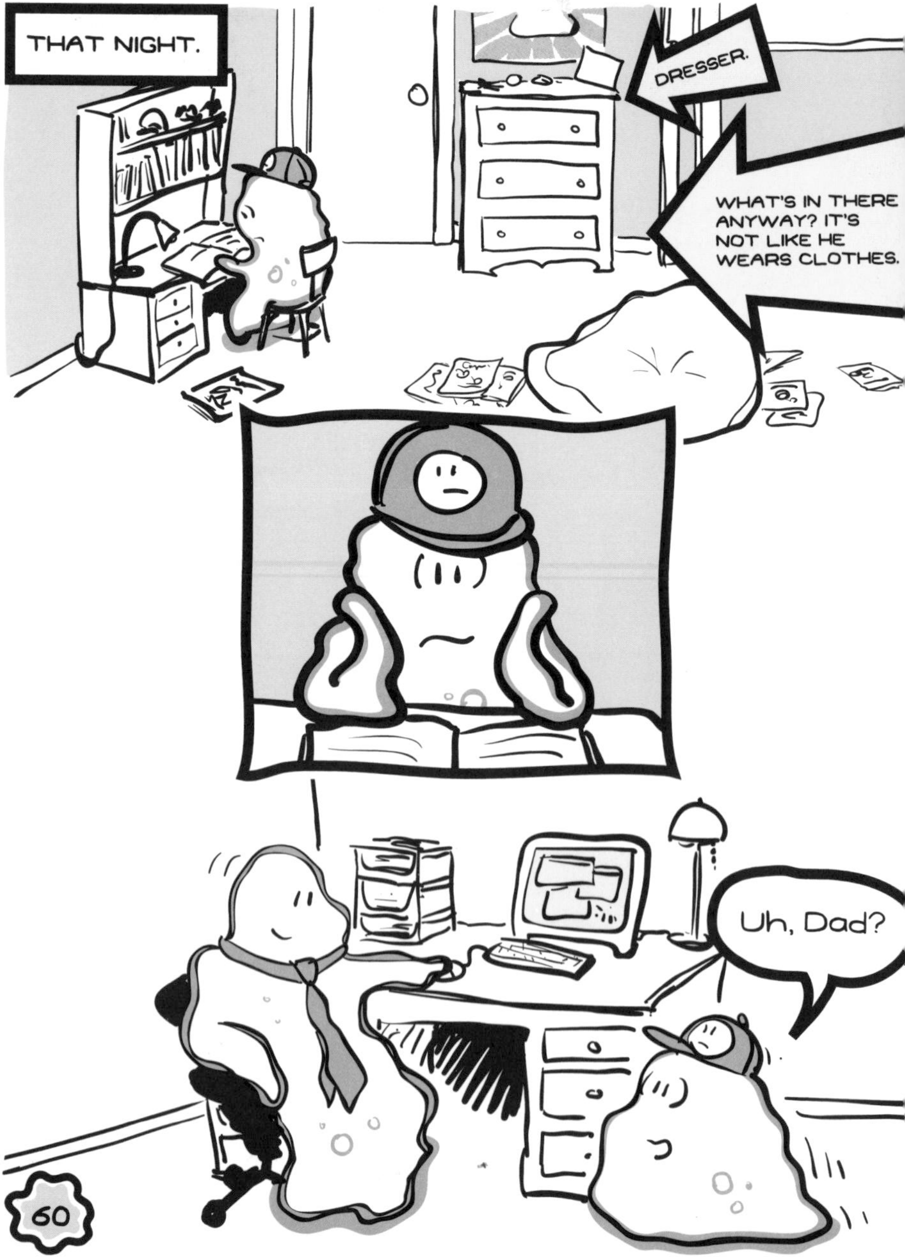
THAT NIGHT.
DRESSER.
WHAT'S IN THERE ANYWAY? IT'S NOT LIKE HE WEARS CLOTHES.
Uh, Dad?

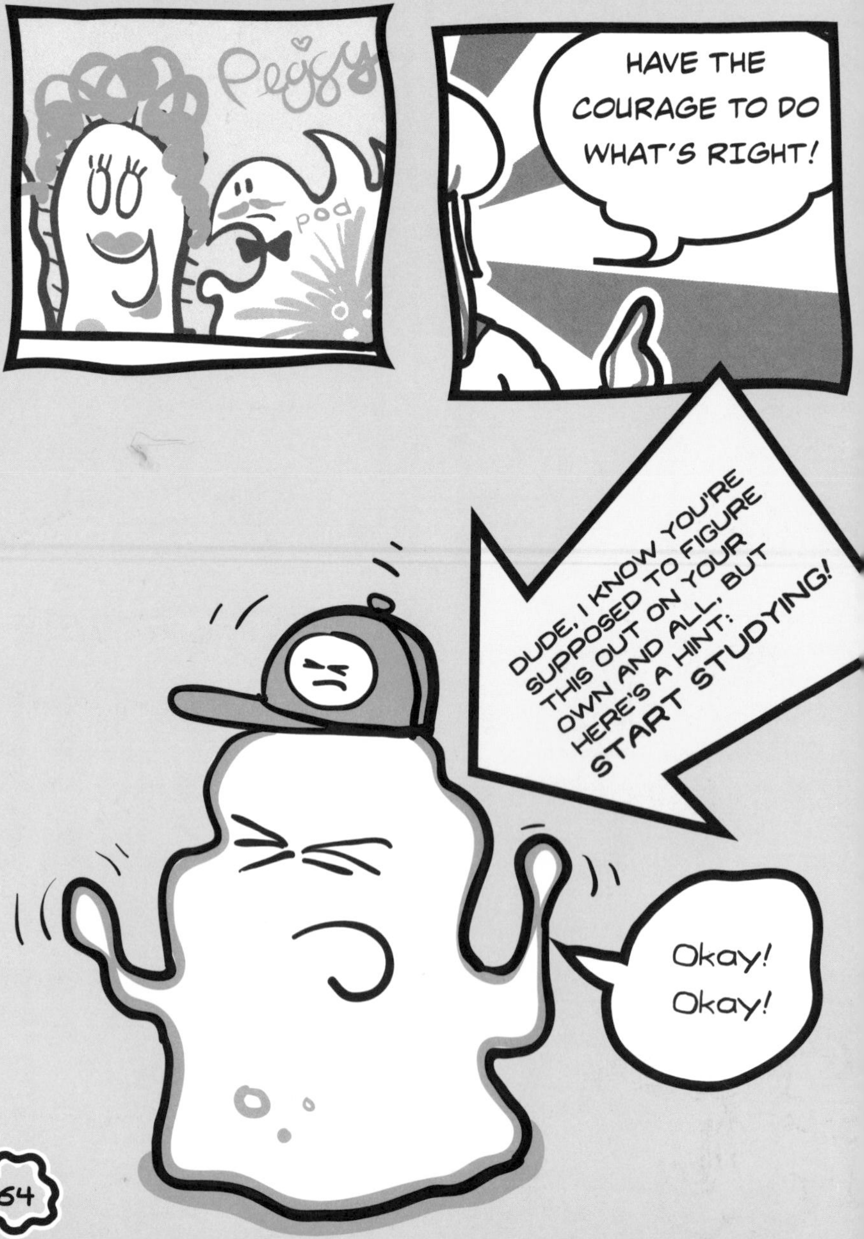
Peggy
pod
HAVE THE COURAGE TO DO WHAT'S RIGHT!
DUDE, I KNOW YOU'RE SUPPOSED TO FIGURE THIS OUT ON YOUR OWN AND ALL, BUT HERE'S A HINT: START STUDYING!
Okay! Okay!

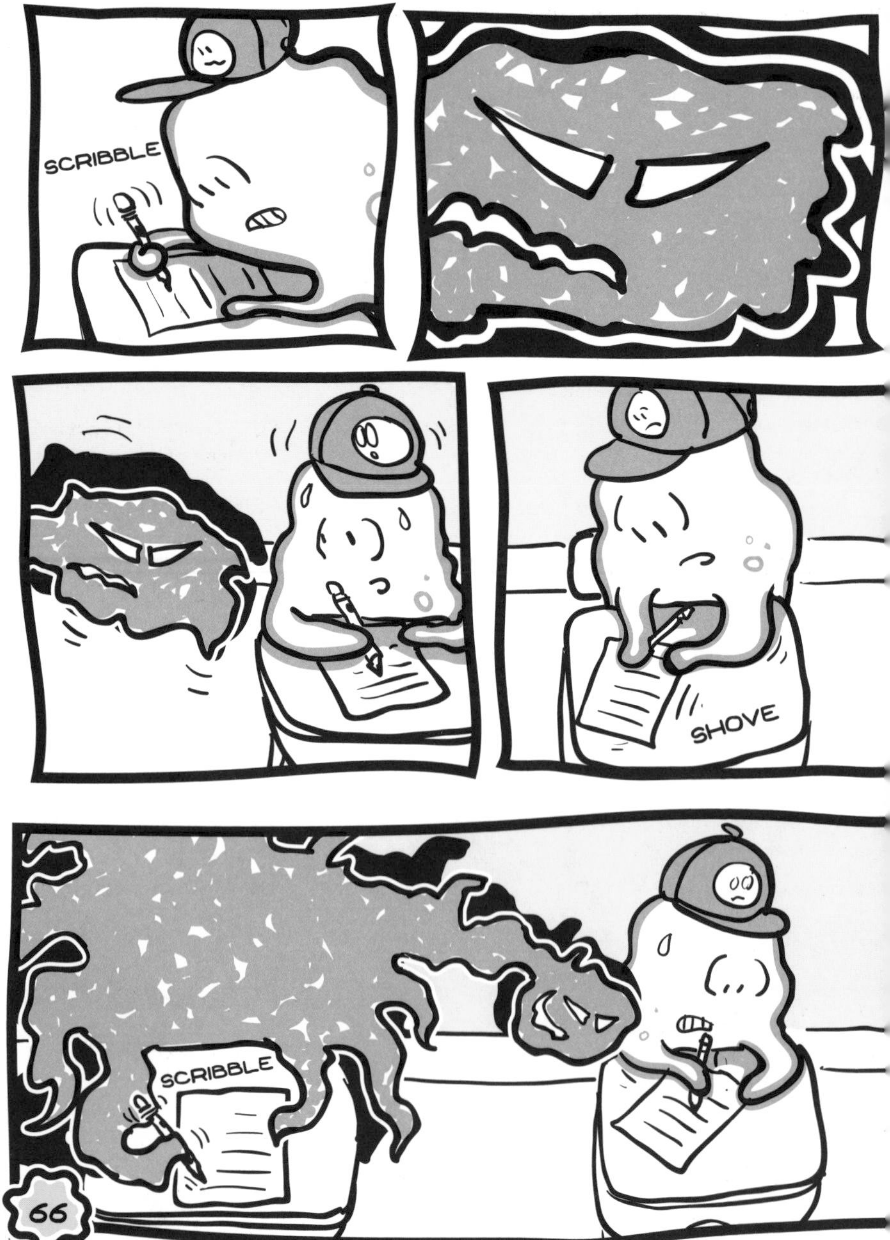
SCRIBBLE
SHOVE
SCRIBBLE

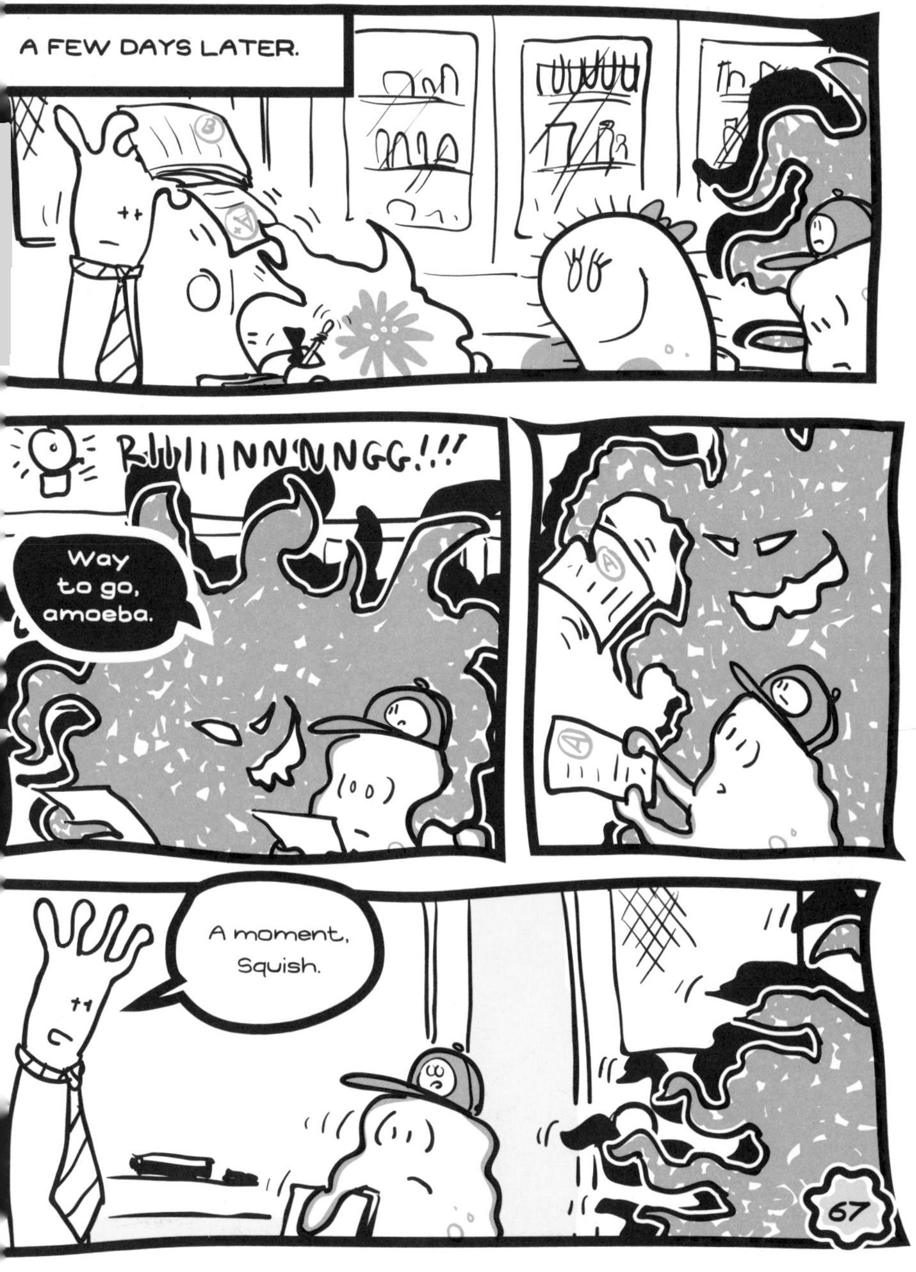
A FEW DAYS LATER.
RIIIIINNNNNGG!!!
Way to go, amoeba.
A moment, Squish.

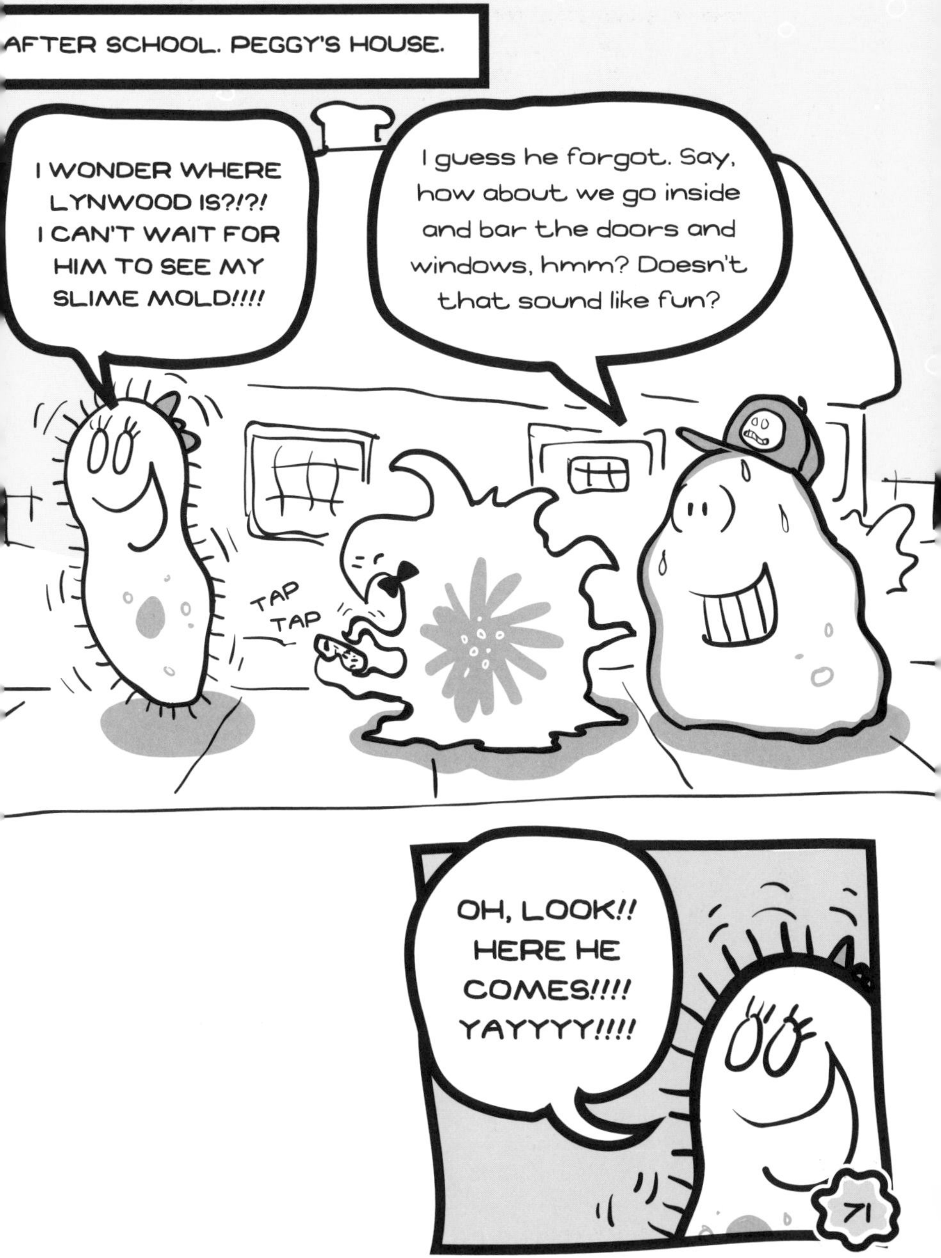
AFTER SCHOOL. PEGGY'S HOUSE.
I WONDER WHERE LYNWOOD IS?!?! I CAN'T WAIT FOR HIM TO SEE MY SLIME MOLD!!!!
I guess he forgot. Say, how about we go inside and bar the doors and windows, hmm? Doesn't that sound like fun?
TAP TAP
OH, LOOK!! HERE HE COMES!!!! YAYYYY!!!!
71

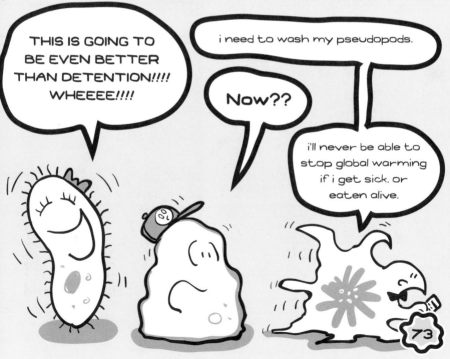

73

TO . . .

SPROING!!!!

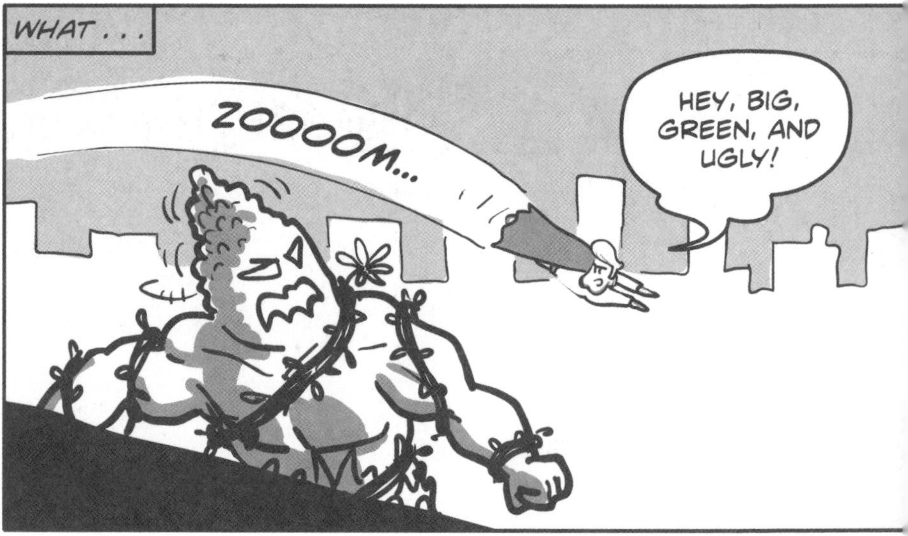
WHAT . . .
ZOOOOOM...
HEY, BIG, GREEN, AND UGLY!

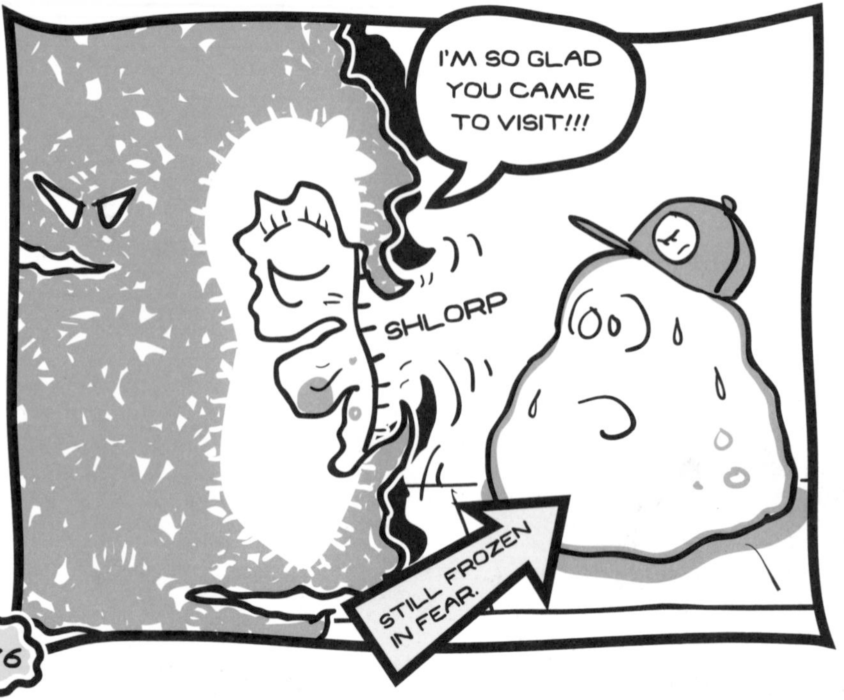
I'M SO GLAD YOU CAME TO VISIT!!!
SHLORP
STILL FROZEN IN FEAR.

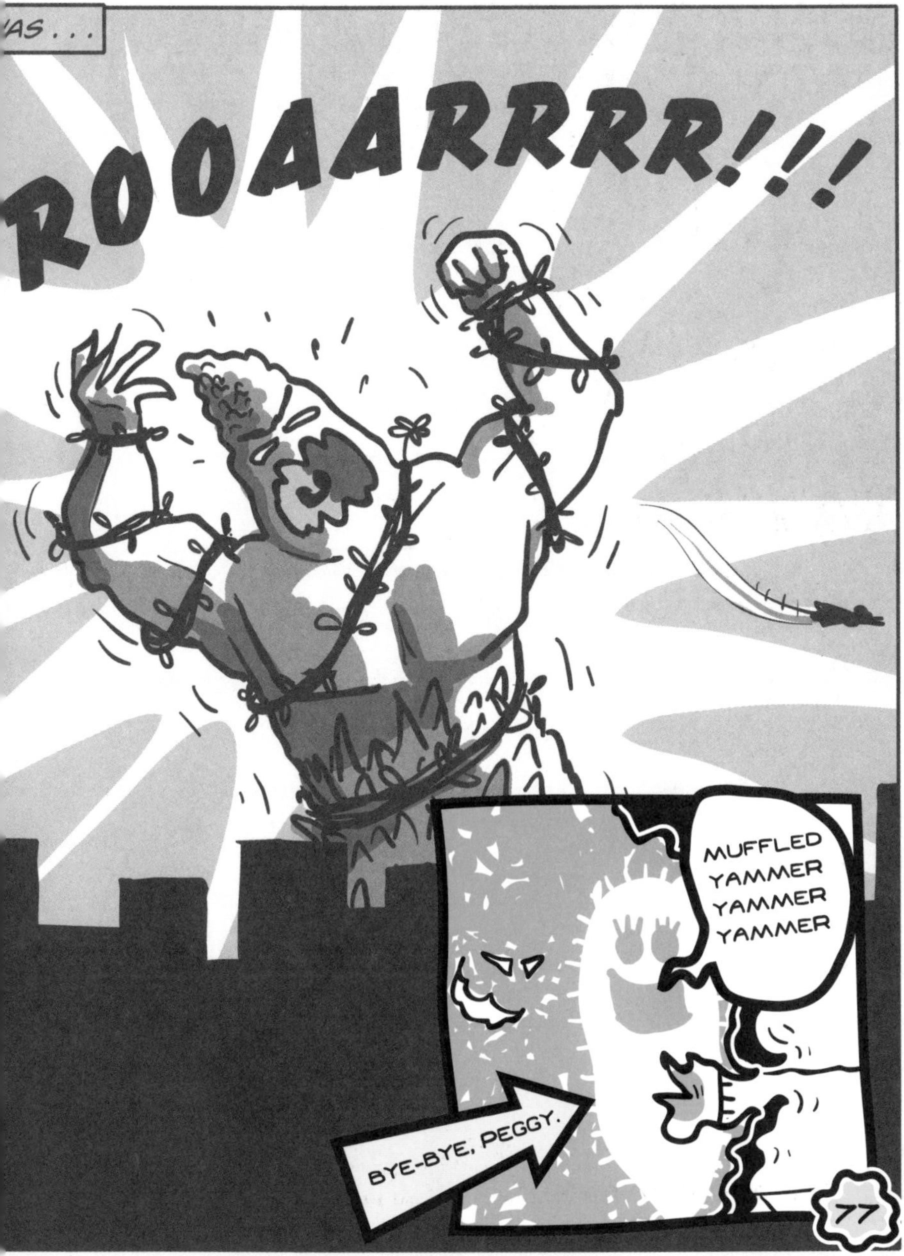

WAS . . .
ROOAARRRRR!!!
MUFFLED YAMMER YAMMER YAMMER
BYE-BYE, PEGGY.

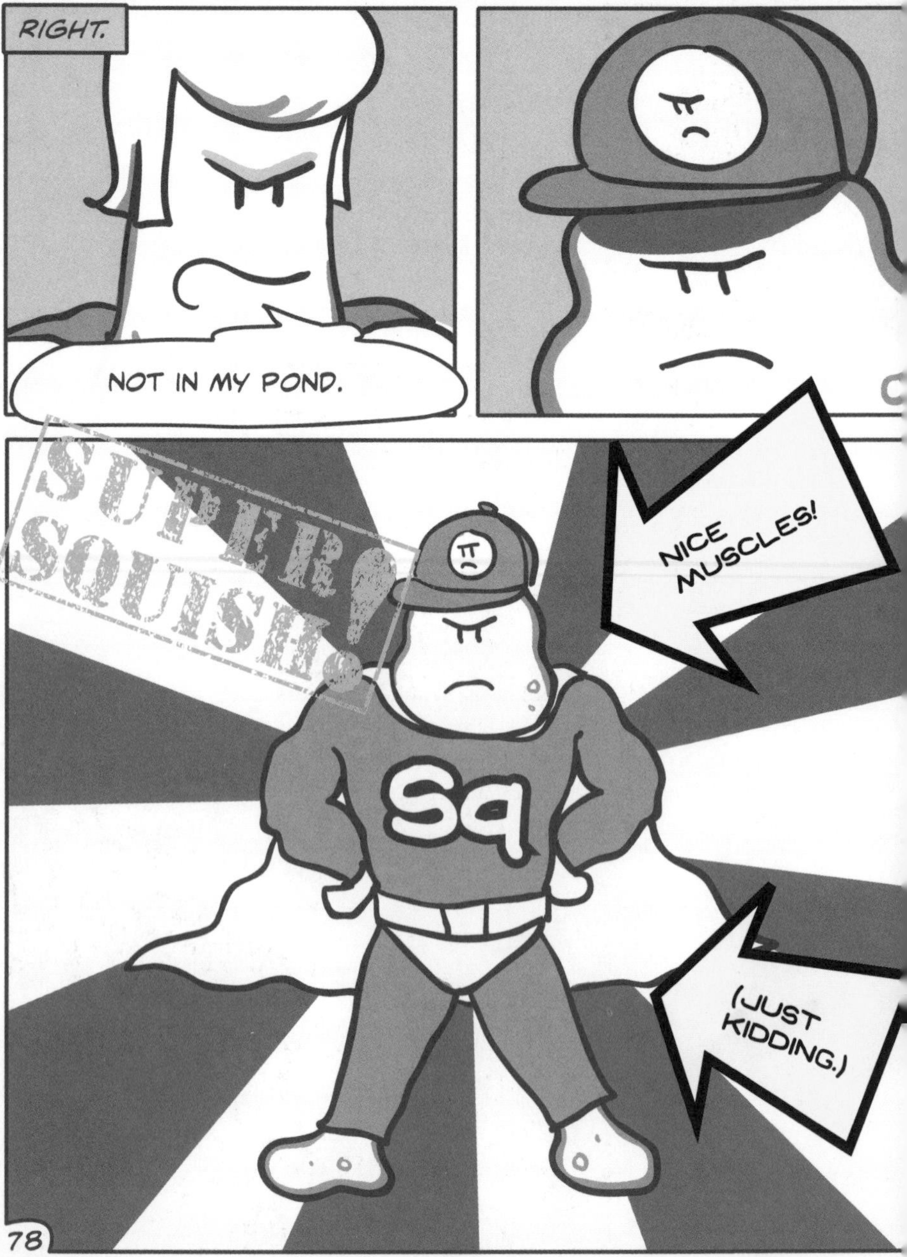
RIGHT.
NOT IN MY POND.
SUPER SQUISH!
NICE MUSCLES!
(JUST KIDDING.)

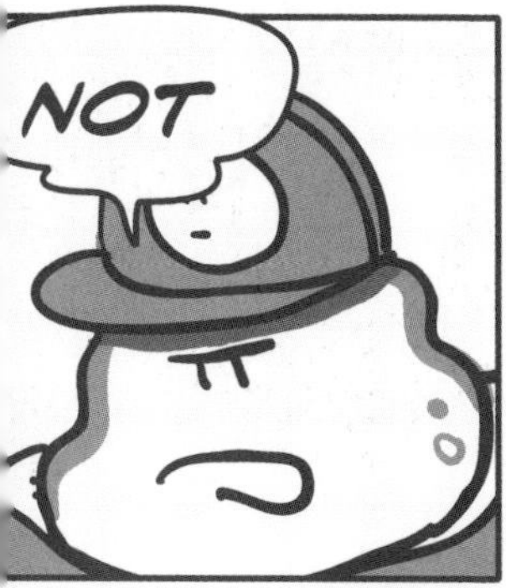
NOT

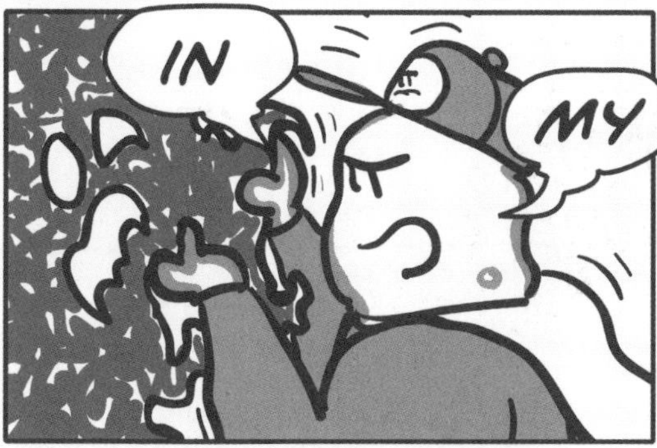
IN
MY

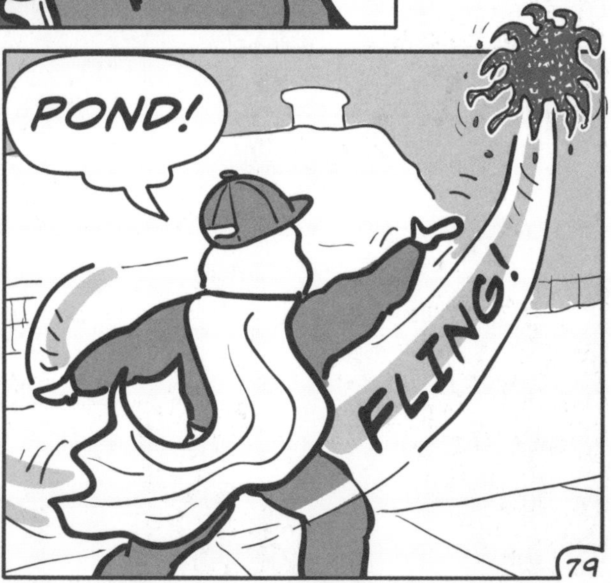
POND!
FLING!

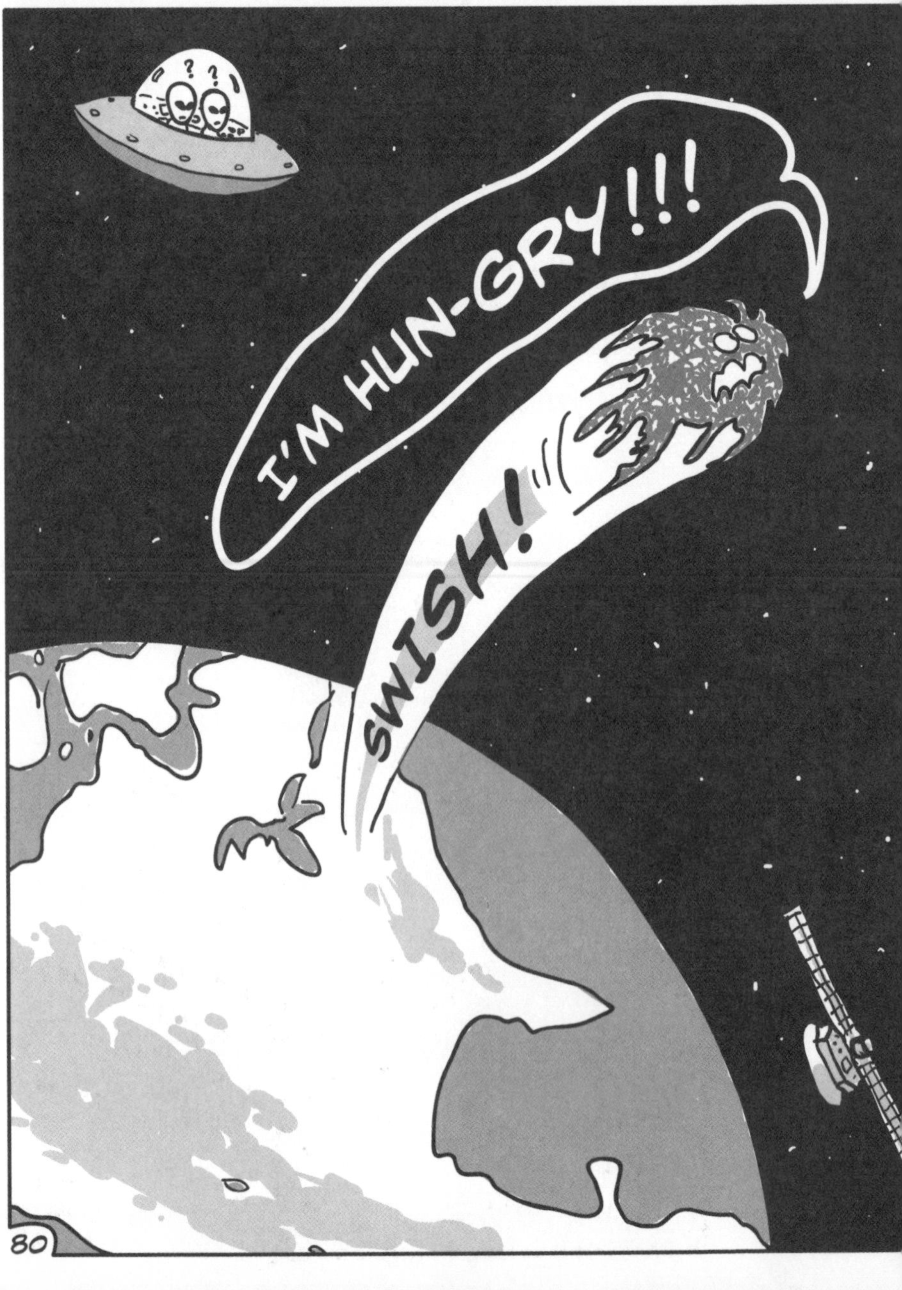
? ?
I'M HUN-GRY!!!
SWISH!

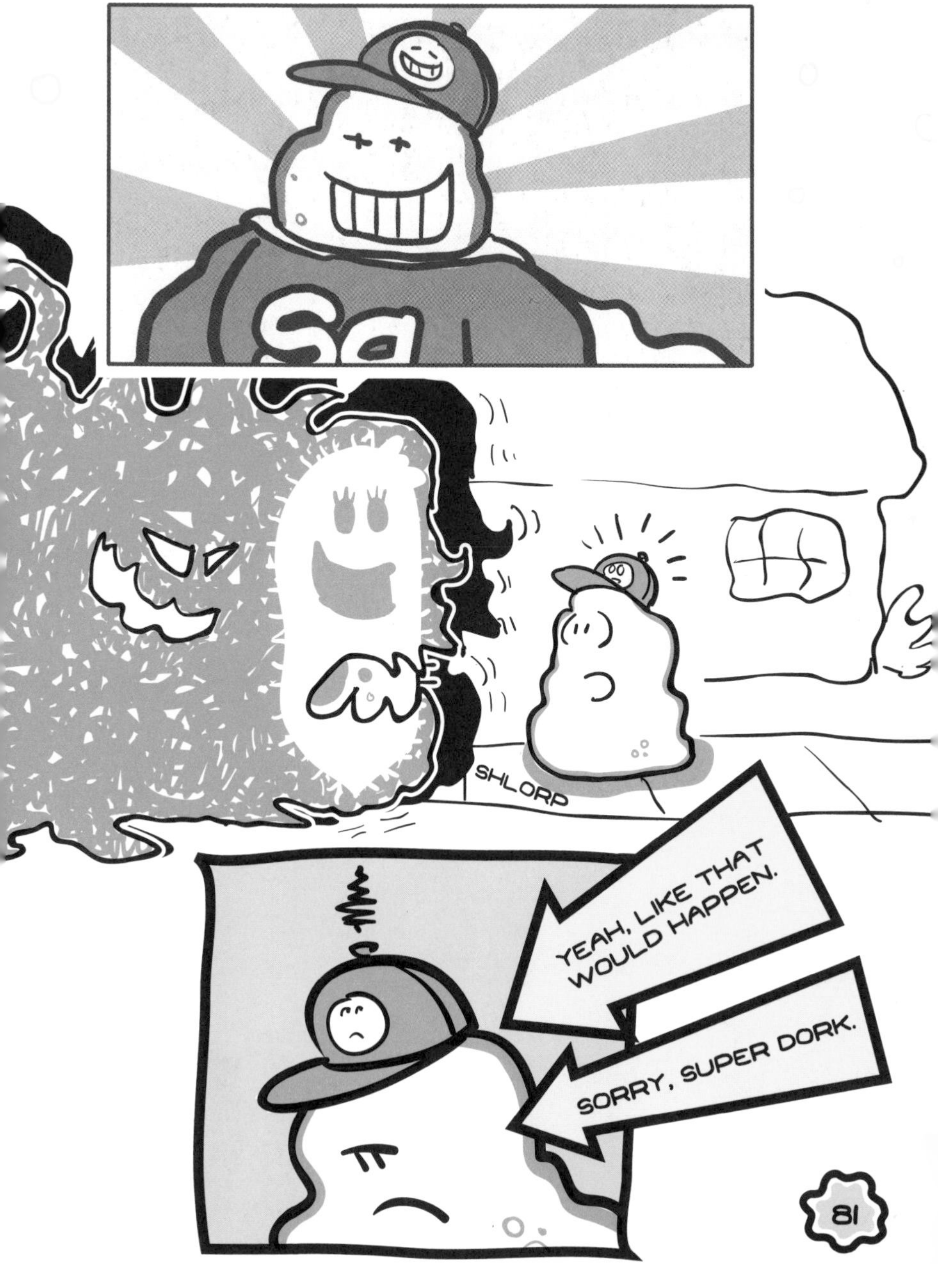

SHLORP
YEAH, LIKE THAT WOULD HAPPEN.
SORRY, SUPER DORK.

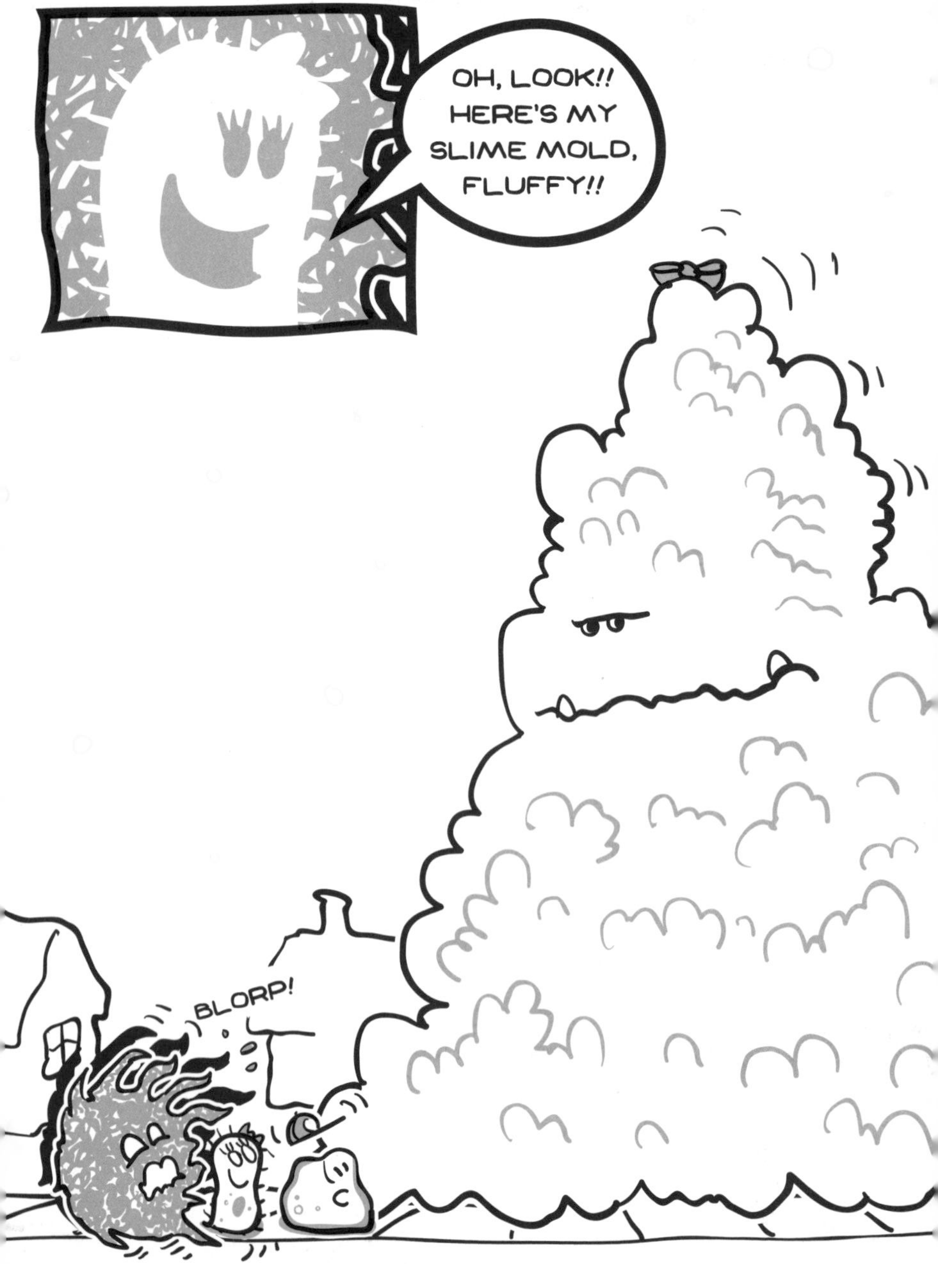
OH, LOOK!! HERE'S MY SLIME MOLD, FLUFFY!!
BLORP!

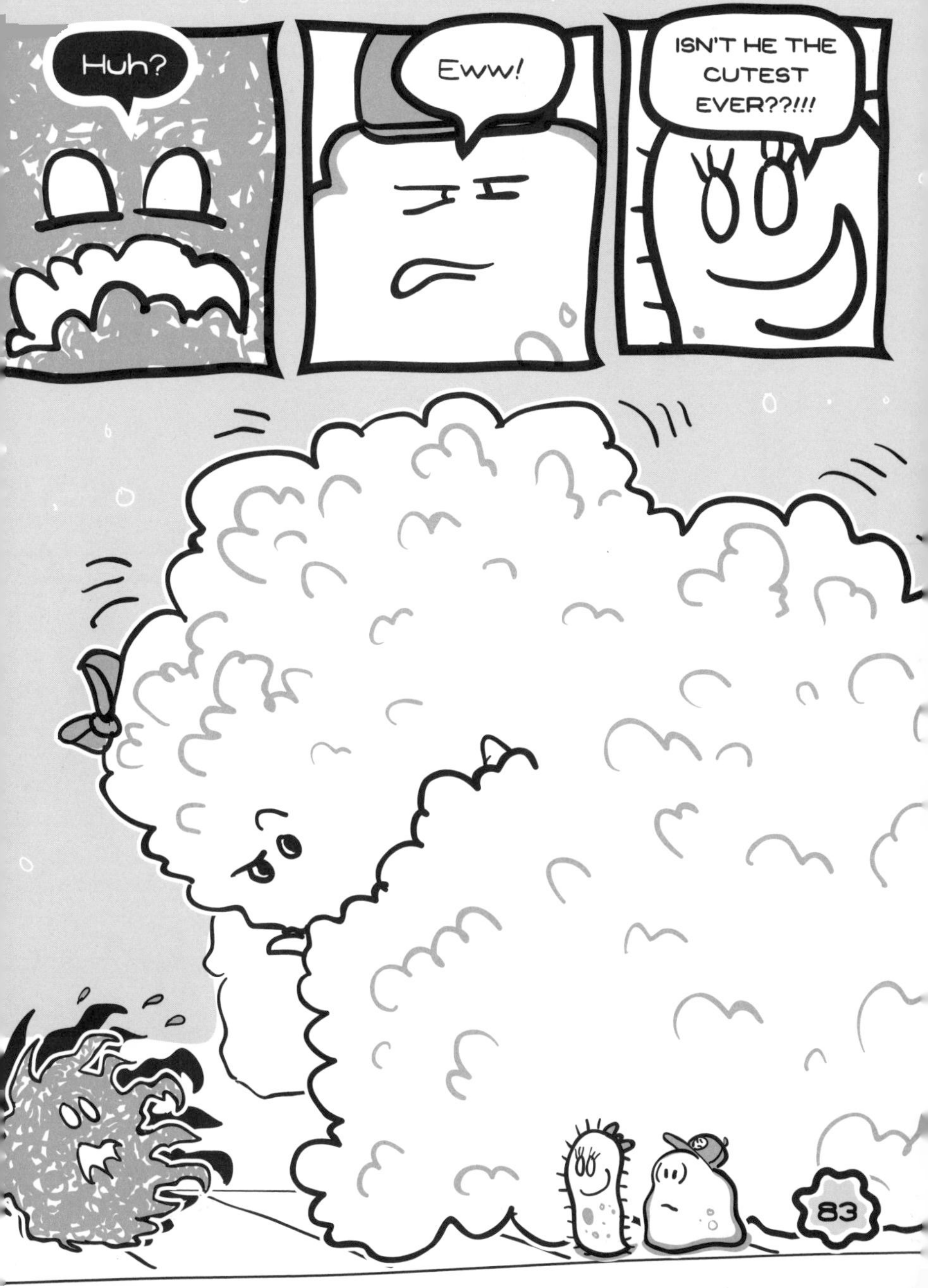
Huh?
Eww!
ISN'T HE THE CUTEST EVER??!!!

GRARH!
GULP!
AAAH-
OH DARN!! HE ATE LYNWOOD!!
Gross!
BURP!
SERIOUSLY GROSS!

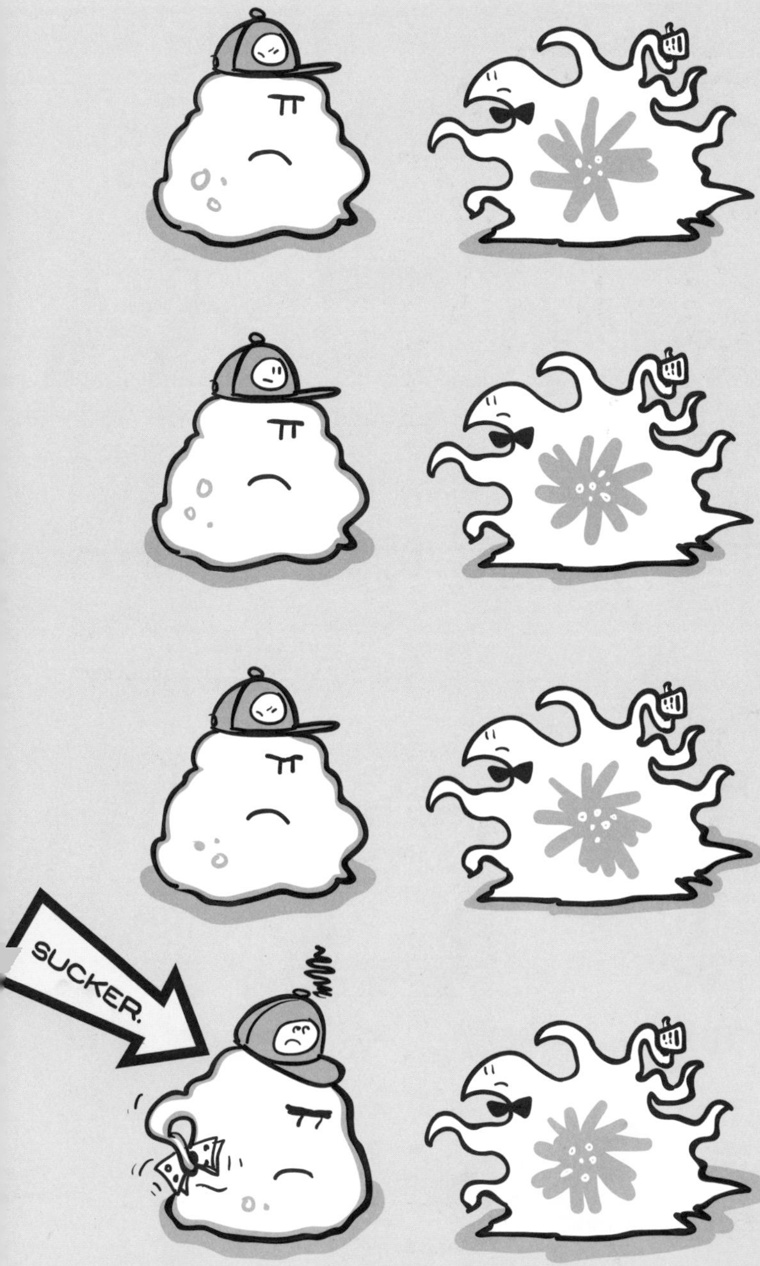
SUCKER.

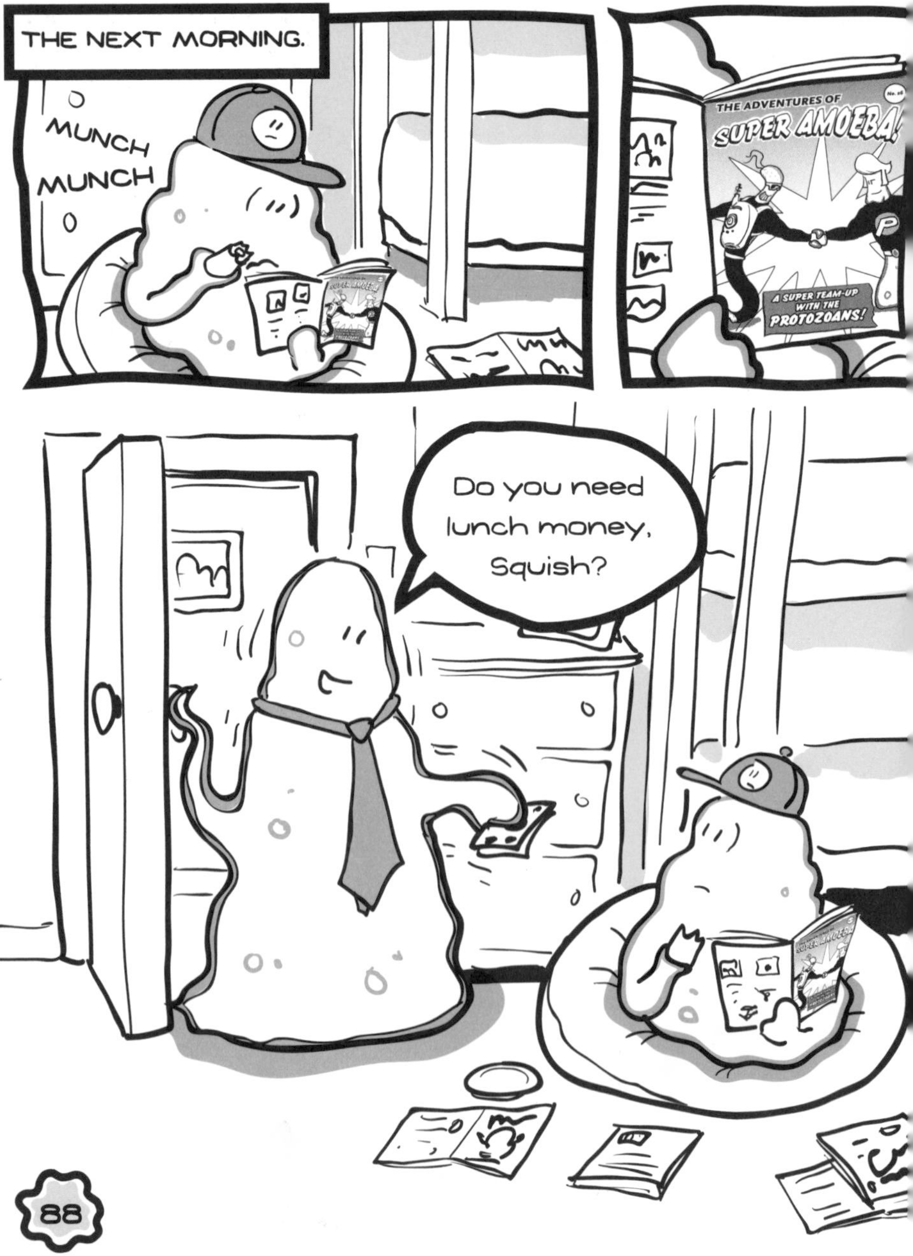
THE NEXT MORNING.
MUNCH
MUNCH
THE ADVENTURES OF
SUPER AMOEBA!
A SUPER TEAM-UP WITH THE PROTOZOANS!
Do you need lunch money, Squish?

89

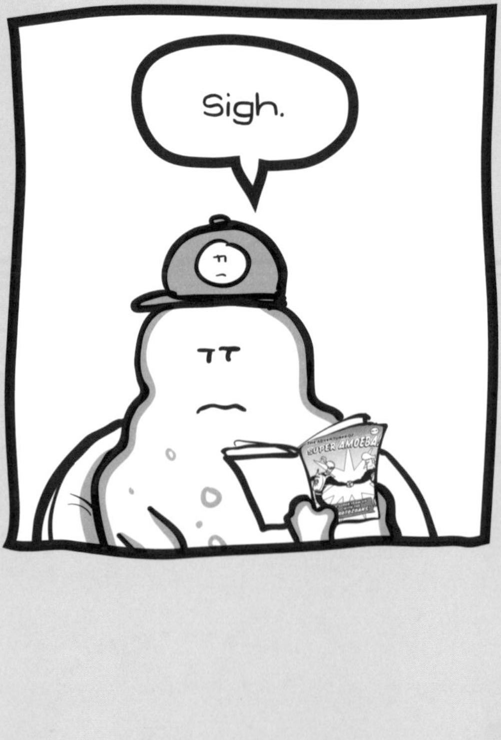
Sigh.
SUPER AMOEBA!

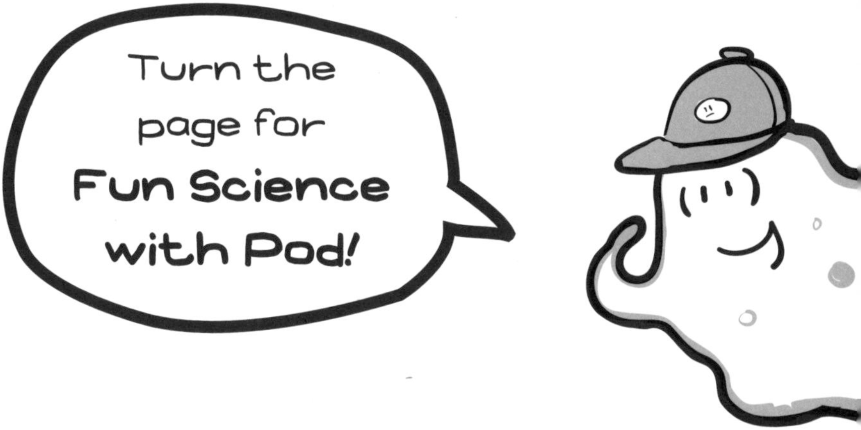
Turn the page for **Fun Science with Pod!**

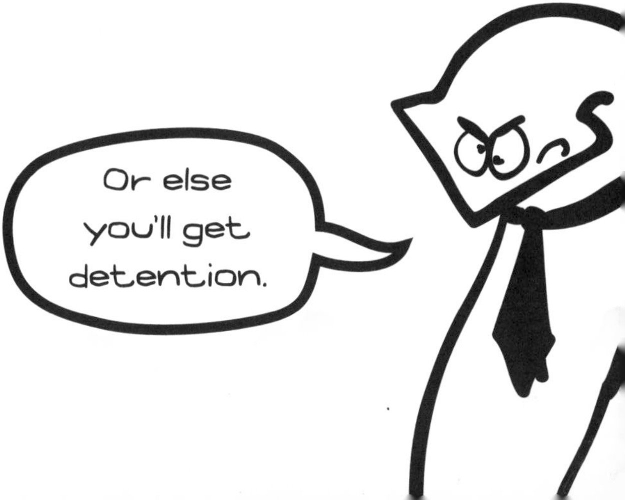
Or else you'll get detention.

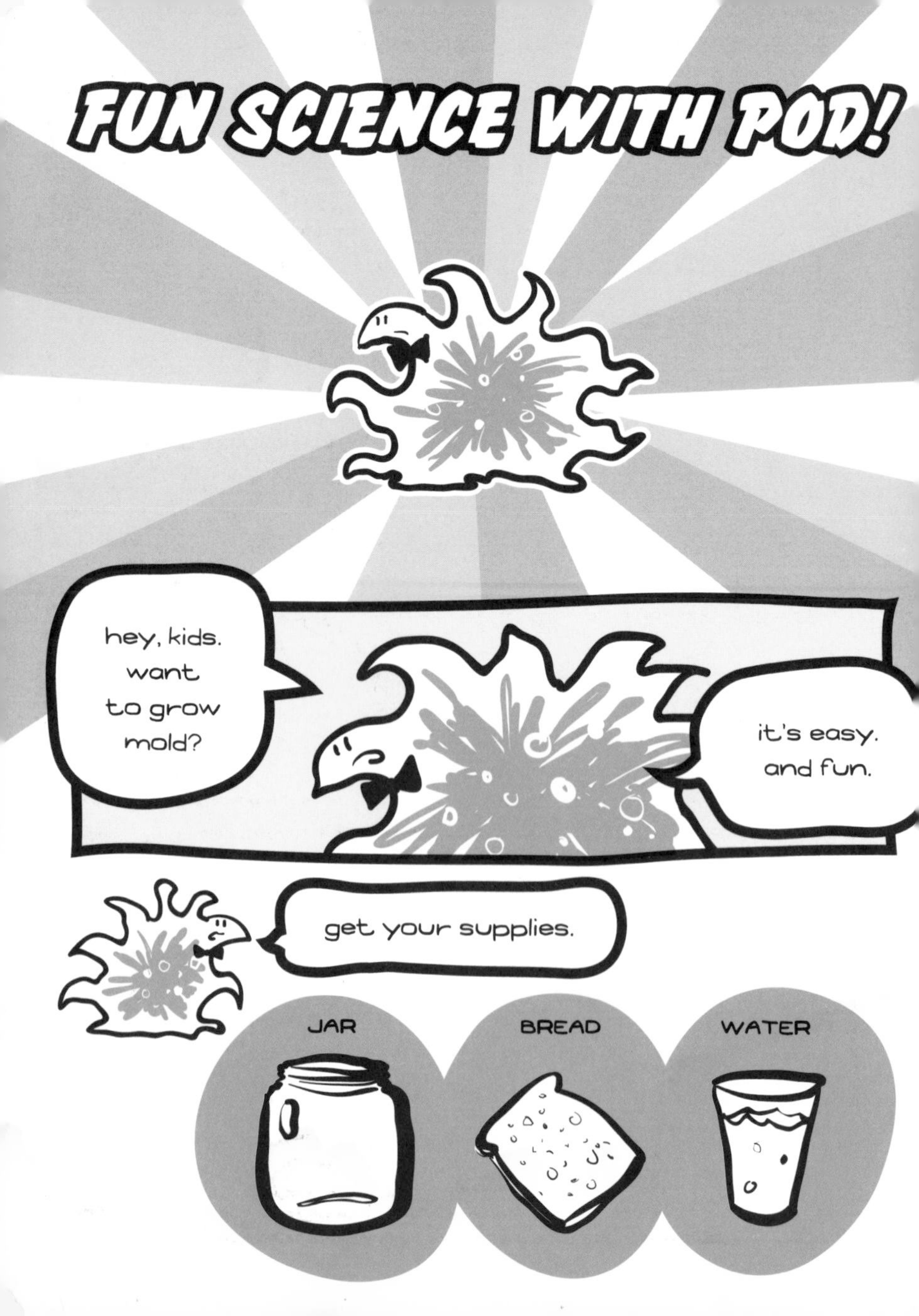
FUN SCIENCE WITH POD!
hey, kids. want to grow mold?
it's easy. and fun.
get your supplies.
JAR
BREAD
WATER

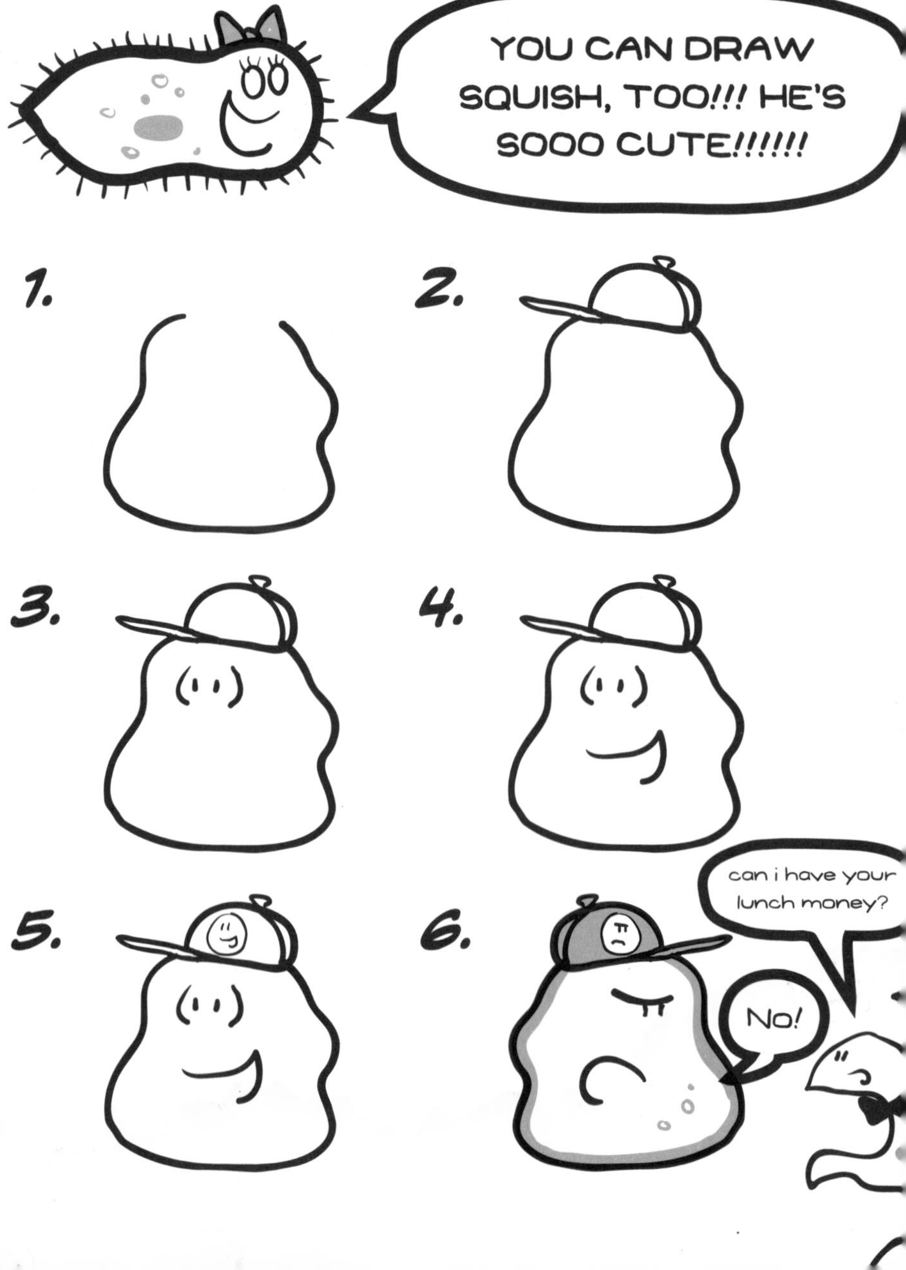
YOU CAN DRAW SQUISH, TOO!!! HE'S SOOO CUTE!!!!!!
1.
2.
3.
4.
5.
6.
can i have your lunch money?
No!

IF YOU LIKE **SQUISH**, YOU'LL LOVE **BABYMOUSE**

#1 BABYMOUSE: Queen of the World!

#2 BABYMOUSE: Our Hero

#3 BABYMOUSE: Beach Babe

#4 BABYMOUSE: Rock Star

#5 BABYMOUSE: Heartbreaker

#6 CAMP BABYMOUSE

#7 BABYMOUSE: Skater Girl

#8 BABYMOUSE: Puppy Love

#9 BABYMOUSE: Monster Mash

#10 BABYMOUSE: The Musical

#11 BABYMOUSE: Dragonslayer

#12 BABYMOUSE: Burns Rubber

#13 BABYMOUSE: Cupcake Tycoon

#14 BABYMOUSE: Mad Scientist

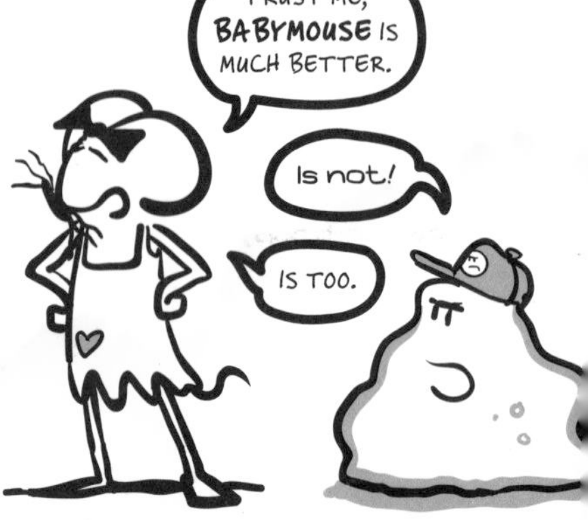
TRUST ME, BABYMOUSE IS MUCH BETTER.
Is not!
IS TOO.